# THE LA

A Novel by
## Stan R. Gregory, Esq.

NEVAEH
PUBLISHING
*www.nevaehpublishing.com*

Nevaeh Publishing, LLC
P.O. Box 962
Redan, GA 30074-0962

ISBN-13: 9780983918752
Library of Congress Control Number: 2011937081

First Printing: January 2012

Printed in the United States of America

# THE LAW CLERK

Stan R. Gregory, Esq.

*With much seductive speech
she persuades him;
        with her smooth talk
she compels him.
All at once he follows her,
        as an ox goes to the
        slaughter,
or as a stag is caught fast
        till an arrow pierces
its entrails;
as a bird rushes into a
        snare;
        he does not know that
it will cost him his life.*

                    Proverbs 7:21-23

*In loving memory of Curtis and Mary Francis Johnson*

# Acknowledgements

I've heard that in order to be a writer, you have to have lived life and have had experiences. You know, meet people and do things so you can feel it when you write it. The below have assisted me in such endeavors, and I'd like to acknowledge them for their roles.

First, I'd like to acknowledge the Creator of the Universe, without whom nothing of substance would be possible. Then, I'd like to acknowledge my wife Nicole, without whom, there would be no Sean and Alyssa.

I'd like to thank Dwan Abrams from Nevaeh Publishing for her faith and steadfastness. May the House of Nevaeh prosper.

I'd like to thank Judge Dilts for being nothing like Judge Pomerance. To Mother, Tot, Glenn, Curtis and James, thanks for just putting up with me. I love you all. Thank you to Marissa Jones and Jessica Barrow-Smith for the edits. I need to acknowledge David Johnston for his extensive time and effort and keyartphoto.com for the cover artwork.

Thanks to Al from Jamison's. Because he knows why, I acknowledge Fred Gibbs, Esquire and his entire family.

Also, I need to acknowledge Charles &

Gina Morrone and Thomas & Effie Donaldson.
Their energy flows from the St. Thomas Law
School days. Of course, love goes out to
the entire Johnson-Moton clan. Thank you to
Michael & Jeanette Colby for helping make
things Cosi in Mt. Laurel.

I also want to acknowledge all of the
judges who could have held me in contempt of
court but did not. God bless you all, even
Judge Call.

Peace, love and hair grease,

Stan R. Gregory

# CHAPTER ONE
Monday. Day 1.
August 2, 2010


A film of perspiration formed a perimeter over the brim of his top lip and like a timid rabbit, the bald man finished, "…and that's really how I lost it all."

A long, long pause ensued.

Rawlings could not believe what he had just heard and as he began to realize the full magnitude of the news, his breathing grew heavier into a huff. The revelation caused his eyes to take on a fire-like blaze and his jaw tightened. Rawlings had a baboon-like face, ugly enough to take one by surprise on first glance. It was rumored that he let his dreadlocked hair droop down over parts of his face to help mask the repulsive effect. It did not work too well. As he considered his response, the vein in his neck pulsed and became dangerously swollen.

The office remained still and silent. Rawlings's second-in-command, Tommy, calmly stood behind him off to the right. From the midst of a stone cold grimace, a grin began to stretch across Tommy's face.

There were two rather large henchmen

by the door. The one to the right, Bowers Kaplan, had a mouth full of cavities with one large shark-like tooth in the front that dominated his complete facial makeup. Peterson St. James had actually given Bowers the nickname "Shark Tooth."

The other henchman, Peterson St. James, was large and wide, like a refrigerator. His neck was as thick as a tree stump.

The bald man sat sock-still and stoic, too terrified to move or say anything. A bead of sweat materialized and meandered its way down his forehead, sliding across his left eyebrow. His eyes were fixed on a spot on the carpet between his feet.

Using all the restraint that he could muster, Rawlings made his way over to the bald man. His walk revealed a troll-like physique. He set his eyes inches from the nose of the bald man, exhibiting a bloodthirsty gaze. So close was he, the bald man ascertained that whatever Rawlings had eaten for lunch had contained a healthy dose of garlic.

Then, as though it were a knee-jerk reaction, Rawlings punched the bald man in his face. A wave of rage flowed through his fist, transferring to the cheek of the bald man. The force of the punch sent the bald man to the floor where he laid for a moment, as if to check to see if he were still alive.

Rawlings hovered over the bald man as he made his way back into the chair. One of the henchmen shook his head as if that were a mistake.

Rawlings, punched the bald man as hard as he could, this time in the back of the head and, again, the bald man slammed into the floor. As if he were providing an encore to the previous blow, Rawlings drove his elbow into the bald man's skull.

The bald man let out a loud muffled bark.

Through his dangling dreadlocks, Rawlings eyed the bald man with contempt. He walked over to the window and gazed across the pristine, calm waters of Biscayne Bay. He rubbed his chin as he paced back and forth, sorting out his thoughts.

Rawlings plopped down into his seat behind his desk and noticed that the bald man still lay on the floor. Tommy seemed lost in thought and the henchmen's eyes widened in disbelief.

Through clenched teeth Rawlings muttered, "Bwoy, git up." Rawlings carried a hard, nasal Jamaican accent. He waited for the lump on the carpet to crawl back into its chair.

Once back in the chair, Rawlings growled, "Listen 'ere, bwoy." His voice was low and his tone angry. He could barely speak. "I like yuh. Ask anybody in tis room. Especially tose two men o'er dere by da door who wan rip yuh lungs out." His accent resonated strong. "Dats why yuh alive right now while we speak. But, bwoy, realize now, I don' like yuh dat much."

Rawlings opened up a drawer, pulled out a 9mm gun and placed it on the desk.

"Dere ain't dat much likin' in da world, bwoy."

The bald man's heartbeat fastened and breathing became difficult.

"I like yuh, bwoy, cause of ya *style*.

Dee way yuh came in 'ere a year ago, and den ask *me* to allow *you* to invest *me* money on da stock market. Ya said yuh could make so much money on da stock market dat I could leave da drug trade forever. Yuh knew who I *was*, yuh knew *me* rules. To make a statement like dat, knowin' who *I* was, knowin' wat *I* would do if he wrong, I say, dat bwoy got balls. Big ones. Same fire dat burn in me, I see in yuh, bwoy."

Rawlings looked back out towards the window and took a deep breath, then glanced back over at Tommy whose face remained cold and hard. He knew what Tommy wanted. Rawlings picked up his gun, cocked the hammer, and moved towards the bald man.

"But dere ain't no amount of likin' enuff in tis world for someone who," Rawlings's voice went out of control, "*loses five-hundred tousand dollars of me money!*" He grabbed the back of the bald man's head with his left hand and put the gun nozzle to his forehead with his right. With a crazed look in his eye, he mumbled out, "Muddafucka, I wan kill ya so bad!"

He pushed the gun on his forehead so hard that the bald man fell off the chair. Rawlings, shaking uncontrollably, jumped down onto the floor next to the bald man, grabbed his chin, and stuck the gun into his mouth. Rawlings's bottom lip trembled and his angst caused the gun to shake against the bald man's teeth, making a rattling noise. The henchmen shifted, steadying their feet in preparation.

Had the Grim Reaper known the intensity of Rawlings's desire to kill, it would've made him blush with pride and nothing would've made him happier. But as bad as Rawlings wanted to see the man's brains splat across his wall to wall carpet, he wanted his money back even more. And Rawlings believed that the bald man had the talent and ingenuity to do it. He just needed the right impetus, and Rawlings felt obliged to give it to him.

All of that aside, Rawlings actually liked the bald man, and that ate him up the most. He saw too much of a young robust and confident Rawlings in the bald man. Rawlings had never seen that in any other person besides himself, ever.

With the gun stuck in the bald man's mouth, Rawlings could hardly make up his mind. Every other second it was, "Kill him, don't kill him."

The inner conflict seemed to push Rawlings to his wit's end.

Rawlings whipped the gun out of his mouth. Shark Tooth shook his head and rubbed the back of his neck as Rawlings hovered over the bald man. The fact that he had not pulled the trigger enraged Rawlings even more. In response, he hit the bald man in the head with the gun butt. The bald man screamed in pain. Tommy smiled.

Rawlings yelled, "Ahhggrrr!"

Halfway back to his desk, the absurdity of the bald man still being alive struck Rawlings, causing his anger to rise to a higher level. Infuriated, he turned around and squatted over the bald man, grabbing his chin tight as an ax handle.

"Listen, bwoy! I give yuh tirty days!

Dats it, no more! Yuh don' have me money in tirty days, I make yuh die real painful, bwoy! Ya no seen pain yet!" Rawlings spoke with such fury that his head shook, making his dreadlocks dance about his face as if he had Medusa's snakes for hair.

"Open ya mout," he demanded, but when the man refused to do so, Rawlings pried his mouth open with his fingers and jammed the gun so deep inside that the man gagged on the barrel. The man choked, kicked, and convulsed, but Rawlings pinned him to the floor by his neck.

"Tirty days!" he reiterated. "And if no money, I'll make yuh regret da day yuh was born. Tink I'm lyin, mon?" He nodded his head at his two henchmen. "Me and ma friends have quite an imaginaysheon."

Rawlings snatched the gun out of his mouth, stood up, then stormed back over to the window.

His breathing was still heavy.

"Now, get out," he said without turning around, "fore me change me mind."

Not wasting any time, the bald man mustered up the strength to get his body off the floor, upright and moving. He took a moment to orient himself, then limped over to the door.

Just as he reached the door, positioned between the two unsettled henchmen, Rawlings stated, "And if yuh tinkin 'bout leavin' Miami and runnin', bwoy, it no work for ya. Or else I not be lettin' yuh leave 'ere alive. Me got eyes erywhere."

Rawlings sat back down. The stakes had been set.

With one single facial expression, Rawlings let him know that there would be no second chances. The bald man understood that as he proceeded toward the door. The henchmen slowly stepped aside to let him through as they towered over him. Walking between them, he humbly exited the room into the hallway.

* * *

In pain, Demetrius walked to the elevator. He pushed the down button next to the sign that read: 34th FLOOR. As the elevator made its descent, he resolved that just as sure as rosebuds know to bloom in early May, he wanted to live. No matter what it took, no matter what he had to do, he was going to live. He tried to gather himself before he reached the ground floor.

He had just been told, come up with $500,000 in one month, or he was going to die. The doors opened into a large, marble floored atrium.

He stepped out and leaned against the wall as he wiped his face and looked into his hand to see if there was any blood. To his surprise, he saw nothing in his palms but sweat. He would have rather seen blood. *Blood,* he thought, *would at least represent a struggle for life.* But his moist and sticky palms only reminded him of fear, emptiness, and the bleak odds of life he now held.

It was then that he knew he had only one option. It was an extreme long shot, based on an elaborate, illegal scheme. He had been planning it for over a year, and he knew it would probably fail.

However, he would die trying, because at
this point, he had nothing to lose.

\* \* \*

Later that day, the two henchmen enjoyed
an early dinner and discussed what they had
watched transpire between Rawlings and the
bald man.

"Man, can you believe that joker
actually walked out of there today?" Shark
Tooth asked with a blank look on his face.

"I don't get it, bro. I'm confused,"
Peterson confessed.

Shark Tooth pressed on, "What's up with
Rawlings, man?"

"I can't call it. I've never seen him
let someone slip through like that. There was
a time when Rawlings would've killed him on
sight for that shit, ya know what I mean?"

Shark Tooth shook his head. "Yeah.
Sheesh."

"I was just waiting for the order,
brother."

"Me too."

Peterson proclaimed in all honesty, "I
would've started by kicking in his teeth and
watched the blood ease out his gums right
across that lying tongue, which, I would have
cut off."

"Ha!" replied Shark Tooth. "I think I
would've snapped his neck, and then, while he
was gasping for air, broken both his legs at
the knee caps. No need for blood, it's too
hard to clean."

"Good one!" Peterson thought that was
just a grand idea.

Many times before they had seen Rawlings give the order to murder for much less than what the bald man had done. The bald man had brought a new level of monetary loss to Rawlings consciousness. Such a loss had not been possibly conceived by Rawlings prior to the bald man's announcement. And the news began to spread through the drug underworld like a viral video of Kim Kardashian through the Internet. So much so that the issue had been dealt with by Rawlings, personally, and everyone knew how it would end.

Peterson and Shark Tooth had sensed that when the bald man arrived Rawlings would cause blood to flow like a mighty river and reach a whole new level in inflicting serious bodily injury and pain. It was always a bloody mess when Rawlings got mad, and it was their job to remove the body and make the office as clean as an operating room.

Peterson and Shark Tooth were experts by now. They had been at it for over twenty years, since Rawlings lit up his first victim in a fit of rage.

The two learned their trade through on-the-job training. They had been originally hired to watch everyone else while Rawlings made highly volatile money-for-drugs exchanges. When the money paid was short by $2,000, Rawlings started popping bullets off into people's chests. When he was done, three men laid dead; all from the other side.

Right there on the scene, Rawlings improvised and appointed Bowers Kaplan, also known as Shark Tooth, and Peterson St. James to dispose of the two bodies—which they did so well that it was like they'd been

disposing of bodies all their lives and had
perfected the craft.

After that, the two henchmen became best
of friends. The disposal of the bodies became
some sort of bonding consummation between the
two of them. They were inseparable. Peterson
and Shark Tooth were in their own fraternity.
They had the privilege of being the people
in charge of disposing of Rawlings's dead
corpses. A growth business.

They did everything and went everywhere
together. Lunch, movies, even vacations. They
looked up to each other and drew strength
from each other. They each thought the other
to be the ultimate henchman. In a fraternal
way, they loved each other, for no one else
could understand the utter importance and
pressure of their job, except themselves.
Proud of their standing in the organization,
Bowers Kaplan and Peterson St. James worked
together with efficiency and diligence.

First they swore their undying
allegiance to Rawlings, then, to each other.
And to them, that was the proper order of
things.

They had surmised that cleaning the
scene of any trace of the bald man's blood
would have been particularly bloody and hard
to remove. However, as much as they hated
cleaning up blood, they understood that it
had to be done.

The rule in Miami, Florida was known to
all. If someone pissed Rawlings off, that
someone was going to die. It was that simple.
The police knew it. Rawlings's employees knew
it. Even Rawlings's family and friends knew
it.

But when he arrived at the meeting, the henchmen figured that no one would understand it more than Demetrius. Before he arrived, the idea of Demetrius walking out of that office alive was about as alien to them as fruit to a carnivore. Such a prospect just did not exist.

"I don't like the boy," Peterson stated.

Shark Tooth replied, "I don't either. But that's not the point, Peterson."

"What's the point?"

"There's more at stake here than liking and hating. There's a business aspect here. Rawlings has a reputation which holds a certain value. People know they can't slip up with Rawlings, or else it's their ass. But news of this has hit the street, dude… it makes Rawlings look bad; it makes the organization look bad, and it makes us look bad."

"Well said, brother."

# CHAPTER TWO
Wednesday. Day 3.
August 4, 2010


Demetrius hadn't eaten anything for two days
and under normal circumstances the smell of
fresh French toast would've had him knee
deep into the plate by now. However, on this
particular morning three large pieces of
French toast sat alone and undisturbed in the
middle of his plate. Traipsing back and forth
in the kitchen he caught a glimpse of himself
in a decorative wall mirror and wondered
if the stress line that had formed on his
forehead would be permanent.

He had just finished telling Katherine
his plan and awaited her response. She
gingerly placed her toast on the bare table
and in a slow, labored manner finished chewing
her mouthful. Stymied, she watched him from
her stool in the kitchen nook as he paced
back and forth rubbing one clenched hand in
the palm of the other. She remained silent
until her eyebrows dropped low when she
asked, "Why do you have to steal the money
from *him* of all people?"

The nausea he had been experiencing for
the past two days seemed to hit him with a

jolt. He found a seat on the stool next to
Katherine and steadied himself while starring
out the window focusing his eyes on nothing
in particular. He lifted his hands in the
air, "Where else can I get that kind of money
in the time that I need it?"

She inched closer to him in her stool.
"I don't care, Dee, rob a bank. Anything
but cross Rawlings again. That is just a
*horrible, horrible* plan."

Being both tired and out of options,
Demetrius blankly stared back at her as he
could feel the reality of the situation
ruminating throughout his whole being. He
realized that Katherine was right. Obtaining
the seed money for his plan from Rawlings, in
order to pay Rawlings back, was insane.

Letting out a huff of air, he responded,
"Kathy, look, I thought of robbing a bank.
Believe me, these knots on my head keep
telling me to stay away from this plan, too."
He pointed to the large knots protruding
from his skull placed there by Rawlings.
"But I've already run every other possible
option through my mind a hundred times now,
especially the bank option, and there are too
many problems with a bank robbery."

"Like, what? What makes robbing
Rawlings more feasible than robbing a bank,
Demetrius?"

"For starters, I may only get five or
ten thousand dollars robbing a bank. I
need something like one hundred and twenty
thousand dollars for the seed money. The
bank bills may be marked. There are cameras
everywhere in a bank. The FBI will come
looking for me. You know, I'm already in the

criminal justice system. I'd be an easy find.

"But with Rawlings, this is black market money. The police won't be as interested in getting involved just because of the fact that it is black market money. And the take should be at least $120,000."

Katherine, rolling her eyes, slid back into her stool and crossed her arms.

Demetrius pleaded, "This isn't just for me. If this plan works, we will *both* be financially set for life."

"I've heard that before," she snapped.

His eyes widened in response. He understood what she was referring to and the thought of it made him wince. In one of his first *plans* to get rich for life, he had lost his seat on the New York Stock Exchange. It was a risky, harebrained, illegal idea he had conjured up. It nearly landed him in jail and left them both flat broke.

Three years later he had worked himself to the position of chief financial officer at a national office supply company. Allegations were leveled against him that he had cooked the books so that the stock value of the company was substantially inflated. In an "agreement" he resigned and in the process, lost $1.1 million in future stock options. It almost landed him in jail, and both he and Katherine were, again, flat broke.

And those were only the results of two of the many *plans* he had concocted.

He decided to simply tell her how it was. "If I don't raise the money, I'm going to die, and I'm scared, Katherine." He felt lost inside, as if he were floating around in outer-space, with no gravity and no clear direction. No up, down, backward or forward. Every option he pondered in his convoluted world had death as a real possible outcome for him. "This really is my best option. I've gotta do it and for my plan to work, I'm going to need your help, again." He framed it as a statement but from the stern tenor of his voice he was ordering her to help.

"Help you? Again?" She put her face down in her hands and her shoulders fell limp. "Shit," she whispered through her fingers.

When she felt his hand on her shoulder she pulled back as if his hand dealt her an electric shock. In surprise he snatched his hand away. In that short moment in time, at last, with his life in the balance, and needing her help more than ever, he actually had empathy for her. But it wasn't much.

Resolutely he said, "Katherine, I've gotta do my part. Can I count on you to do yours? You know what I'm going to need you to do."

She knew all too well. She sat there, silent.

His watch read 8:27 a.m. which meant he had to get moving relatively soon, if his plan was going to stay on schedule. He whispered to her, "Kathy, I need to go do this *thing* in a few minutes. My window of opportunity is quickly closing. So, I need to know, can I count on you to do your part?"

When she didn't respond, he began to think about the last time she told Demetrius that she wasn't going to help him. For her own sake, he hoped that she was thinking about the same thing. He would hate to go through that exercise again. He tilted his

head down and squeezed his eyes shut hoping
for the right response.

Through her hands she let out a muffled,
"Demetrius, I always *help* you, don't I?"

Demetrius opened his eyes and looked
at her. "Thank you, babe." He exited the
kitchen, grabbing his Glock nine millimeter
handgun off the table, stuffing it into the
front of his belt. Stopping at the door to
the apartment he turned and with what sounded
like real gratitude in his voice said, "Babe,
I love you."

She kept her hands in her face and when
she failed to respond, he gently shut the
door behind him.

* * *

His watch read 9:52 a.m. and he knew
that the van would soon be there. Like a
football player mentally preparing himself to
run out onto the field from the locker room,
Demetrius forced himself to only imagine one
outcome—victory. He paced in a small circle
as he mumbled his mantra to himself, over and
over again, "I cannot lose. I cannot lose."

Pulling a fat-assed marijuana cigarette
out of his pants pocket he repeated his
mantra, "I cannot lose, I cannot lose." He
lit the joint and drew a long deep drag into
his lungs. He held the hemp smoke inside him
for as long as he could before exhaling the
smoky haze into the atmosphere.

He repeated the mantra until the joint
was all smoked up. A joint of that size
might have incapacitated the average man,
but Demetrius had been smoking weed off and

on since he was eleven years old. This is
what he did when he needed to loosen up while
staying focused.

While waiting for the full *marijuana
effect* to take hold Demetrius took stock
of why he had come to Liberty City this
morning—to rob Rawlings blind.

He stood in a small alley across the
street from Mr. G's Barbershop, hidden from
the public eye, on the corner of 7th Avenue
and 63rd Street. He was in the Liberty City
section of Miami, run down, poor, and a haven
for drug trafficking.

He leaned his back against the wall of
a building. Peeping around the corner of the
building to across the street he eyed the
storefronts abutting either side of Mr.G's.
On one side stood a liquor store, on the
other, The First Holy Apocalyptic Church of
Love. The storefronts were surrounded by
boarded up buildings and weed infested lots
that seemed to invade every empty nook and
cranny of Liberty City.

After waiting a few minutes, the full
marijuana effect took hold. He felt his
shoulder muscles relax. The colors around him
seemed more vivid. Everything in the universe
seemed to fall into its proper place for him.
He began to feel comfortable in his skin and
whole as a human being.

He mumbled to himself, "This is it,
dude. This is real." He smiled although he
knew the odds were that he was about to
die, but somehow in that moment, he felt
free. He now faced a test with his back to
the wall and the only possible way he could
succeed was if he were to push himself to his

absolute limit. He almost felt orgasmic at the prospect.

*Now, this is what life's about,* he thought as he felt a fire grow in his belly. An unexplainable rush overtook him as goose bumps ran through his back and arms. He glared in the direction of the barbershop and quietly, with conviction repeated, "I cannot lose, I cannot lose."

From months of being so close to Rawlings he knew that the cash pick up for Liberty City was always on Wednesday morning, ten o'clock at the barbershop on the corner of 7th Avenue and 63rd Street. And since the past weekend had been a welfare paycheck weekend, he was keenly aware that today's take could be well above average.

Helping to conceal his face as well as his bald head he pulled his New York Yankee hat down low over his eyes. Feigning a yawn and rub of his stomach he reached under his baggy shirt to confirm that his gun was tightly secured in his waist belt.

A tingling feeling drew his attention to his forearm where he saw a small butterfly resting. With a snap of his wrist he smashed the butterfly under his palm. He flicked its mangled wings and torso off his arm and onto the sidewalk.

His attention was brought back across the street when, like clockwork, at 10:03, a dark blue van with no side windows arrived in front of the barbershop.

Through the driver's side window Demetrius could see the driver. It was Bowers Kaplan, aka Shark Tooth. At the sight he began to clench his teeth until his gums hurt.

Staying safely cloaked across the street Demetrius watched as two men stepped out of the sliding side door of the van. One was tall and muscular, with a juicy Prince and the Revolution type Jheri curl. The man took a final drag from a cigarette, tossed it onto the ground and extinguished it under his foot. Demetrius had seen him at some of the meetings with Rawlings and knew him only as Joshua. The other, was a portly Cuban, with dark black hair. Demetrius recognized him as Fermin, who like Joshua was a low-level associate in Rawlings's organization.

After they exited the van, they made a brief survey of their surroundings, taking a quick 360 for anything that might look unusual to them. Demetrius darted his head back around the corner when they scanned his direction. Shortly thereafter, they vanished into the barbershop.

Demetrius waited for them to come back out while tapping his index finger against the wall. "Come on, come on," he said under his breath, eyes sharply fixed on the door. As he waited time seemed to move with an evolutionary slowness. To Demetrius it felt like generations of new species could have evolved in the time that it took the two men to exit the barbershop. In reality, it was only three minutes later when the first man appeared.

It was Fermin, carrying a large canvas bag.

"Cash money, baby," Demetrius said to himself. "You're coming home with me tonight."

Fermin put the cash into the van then looked around, scanning the environment. Demetrius bobbed his head back around the corner. Seeing nothing unusual, Fermin got into the van, sliding the door closed behind him.

Then, nothing happened. Time again slowed, to almost moving backwards in Demetrius's mind.

"Damn it all," Demetrius said as he looked across the street. "Where's the other guy?" He could feel his blood trying to run hot. "Be cool, Dee," he reflected to himself. "I cannot lose."

Again, time seemed to move as slow as drying paint for Demetrius. Readjusting his hat and rubbing his hidden gun for the tenth time he leaned his back against the wall and continued his peer at the barbershop door.

Two species later, Joshua walked out of the barbershop, smoking a cigarette, carrying a canvas bag similar to the one carried by Fermin. As Joshua came within ten feet of the van door, Demetrius struck out across the street in a full sprint. He approached from behind Joshua, and as he got closer, he pulled his gun from under his belt.

Joshua opened the door and threw the canvas bag in. As he lifted his left foot up to enter the van, Demetrius came up directly behind him. In one swift move he shoved Joshua in the back with his left hand while simultaneously shooting him in the back of the head with the gun that he held in his right.

Joshua felt a hand pushing him on his back and heard a loud pop behind him which would be the last sound he would ever hear.

Fermin, who was sitting in the back row seat had his attention drawn to the situation when he heard the pop of the gun. He looked up to see Joshua's brain matter splatter against the far wall of the van and first row seat. Then he saw Joshua's limp body gruffly fall to the floor of the van. With no gun on him Fermin immediately took cover by lying down in the third row seat.

Demetrius could feel the adrenaline pulse through his veins like fire ripping through a dry Arizona pine forest on a windswept day. As soon as Joshua's body hit the ground, as if he were a cat, he nimbly climbed over Joshua's shaking and convulsing body and dove into the van's second row seat.

Bowers, still in the driver's seat, had been playing Pac-Man on his cell phone when he heard the gun pop and thump of Joshua's body. The popping sound of the gun caused him to duck down low in his seat and take cover. By the time he had the courage to glance into the back of the van, all he saw was Joshua's convulsing bloody body on the floor by the open door. He peripherally saw someone leap into the second row seat.

Before Bowers could get any type of understanding as to what was happening or what to do, fear advised him to immediately put the van in drive and mash the pedal all the way to the floor. And he did. The tires screamed like a banshee as the van shot off down 7th Avenue.

Bowers, glancing in to the rearview mirror, yelled through a quivering voice, "Fermin!"

There was no response. Bowers could only hear a scant yelp ruminating from the back of the van. He glanced over his shoulder and saw Joshua's twisted and contorted body in pool of blood.

"Fermin, you alive, man? Talk to me!" His voice was three octaves higher than normal as he felt a sliver of his bowels begin to slip down his pant leg. Under his heavy foot, the van had reached 100 MPH in 25 MPH zone, zipping in and out of traffic.

Bowers screaming like a maniac hollered, "Fermin, what the fuck is going on?" All the while, he was fumbling for the gun under his seat, which he eventually found and placed on his lap. Bowers glanced back over his shoulder where he could see that a fire had begun to grow on the first row seat from Joshua's cigarette. He screamed, "God, help me!" Perspiration flowed from his pores, finding its way into his eyes. He squinted his eyes to ease the sting. Dodging in and out of traffic, he yelled, "Who da fuck is back there? Do you know who you're fuckin' with, son?"

Frantically peering into the rearview mirror, he couldn't see what the hell was going on through all the smoke. When he diverted his eyes back to the road, he saw that he was headed for a car double-parked poking out into his lane of travel. He yanked the steering wheel hard to the left to avoid the car, the force of which tossed Joshua's body out of the van through the open sliding door.

Joshua's body banged hard against the asphalt and tumbled like a rag doll down 7th

Avenue until colliding with the front of a dump truck. His skull cracked open like a dropped watermelon. The dump truck dragged his body under the chassis for another two hundred feet before coming to a stop. The roadway peeled the skin off his body as if it were a cornhusk.

Mournful for his friend, and scared for his own life, Bowers yelled, "God help me!"

Demetrius, lying down in the second row seat, gathered himself trying to figure out how he was going to get out of this mess. He peeked his eyes quickly over the back of his seat, then squatted back down quickly. When he realized no one had taken shot at him, he took another quick peek, this time a little longer.

To his surprise he saw Fermin on the seat, laying down, in a fetal position, crying. His cry was a loud, lamenting scowl that sounded like a screaming cat when stuck at the top of a tree.

Bowers caught a glimpse of Demetrius when he popped his head up to get a second look at Fermin. At the sight of this yet unidentified intruder Bowers grabbed his gun and started firing wildly over his shoulder into the back of the van, screaming, "Die, motherfucker! Die!"

Shielded by the back of the first row seat Demetrius waited for a lull in Bowers's gunfire. He then sat up in his seat, and blasted away. One shot hit Bowers in the shoulder causing him to lose control of the van. The van approached 41st Street where 7th Avenue bears to the left under the Interstate 95 overpass. Bowers, in too much pain, failed to negotiate the turn and the van veered off the road, slamming into the brick wall of a building.

The force of the crash thrust Demetrius against the back of the first row seat and with a thump, down onto the floor. Stunned and with blank eyes he gazed around. His hearing went quiet and Demetrius lay there on the floor of the van filling up with smoke, wondering where he was.

Everything looked blurry, leaving him confused and befuddled. Struggling to breathe, he wallowed back and forth on the floor. *Advil,* he thought as he rubbed his skull. "If I could just have a glass of water and three Advil."

The place was smoky, and as his hearing began to return he started to hear something that he recognized as a screaming cat. Everything around him looked familiar but didn't seem real. *I must be dreaming,* he thought to himself.

Shaking his head to remove the cobwebs, it slowly started coming back to him. With his head still ringing from the collision, instincts caused him to grab his gun off the floor and check to make sure it was loaded.

After a rather long ten to fifteen seconds his brain cleared and in a rush it all came back to him, and he knew where he was. He looked under the seat and saw Fermin on the floor, still in a fetal position, crying and howling.

A thought hit him, *Bowers. I've gotta check Bowers.* He picked himself off the floor to look over the front row seat. He saw that Bowers's head was half through the windshield, and his body was lifeless. At the sight of Bowers's lifeless body Demetrius felt his adrenaline rush begin to ease. He looked back over into the third row seat to find that Fermin hadn't moved.

Gun in hand, looking down on Fermin from the back of the second row seat Demetrius thought, *He's in shock.*

Fermin's cat cry had morphed even louder, now into what Demetrius thought of as a pig squeal.

*He looks pitiful,* Demetrius thought as he wrinkled his face in sorrow for the guy. *I don't want to kill him. He's harmless, and I know he has children.*

Knowing that Fermin would tell Rawlings everything he thought better of it.

As if asking for forgiveness he whispered, "Sorry." Then he pointed his gun at Fermin's head and fired, twice. With that, the pig squeal ceased.

Demetrius understood that with the trail of carnage that had just been created time was short and a crowd of people and police would be on the scene soon. He knew he had to get the money and get moving…now.

Looking out of the open van sliding door he noticed the van had crashed into an abandoned building, in an abandoned lot in one of the many desolate uninhibited pockets of Liberty City. He grabbed the bags of money and struggled with them 75 yards down a small alley so that he was out of sight of the accident scene. Then he hailed a cab.

Thirty-two minutes later, two nonchalant police officers arrived at the scene of the accident. By then, the van and all its contents had been burned to a crisp.

\* \* \*

Safe at home and no longer under the
effects of the marijuana, the bald man opened
the bags and counted the money. When he
finished, his laughter filled the room, for
the bags had contained a little more than
$200,000.

*Morality is a private and costly luxury.*
~Henry Brooks Adams

# CHAPTER THREE
Friday. Day 5.
August 5, 2010

"I'm getting married in two months, Ben. This is one of the few times that you, Thomas, and I are going to be able to hang out. It's not like I'm asking you to go to the club with us. Just come to Rick's with us, throw back a few brews, and get some dinner—"

"Chalie, I really wish I could join you guys," Ben cut his friend off, still banging away at his computer keyboard, "but I still have some motions I need to finish up and—"

"Don't be a squid. It's Friday, Ben. Those motions will still be waiting on you when you get back on Monday morning." When Ben still didn't say anything, Chalie moaned into the phone, "Come on, bro. Thomas hasn't seen you since we graduated from law school. It's like you got hired as a law clerk, went into the courthouse, and died."

Ben couldn't help but laugh at his friend. He knew Chalie was joking, but he was half-serious too. He had been Judge Pomerance's law clerk for eleven months now and had a little less than one month left before his clerkship ended. For the past eleven months as a law clerk, Ben had been a six-to-seven-day-a-week-machine, so he considered weekends to be nothing more than an extension of his workweek. On more than one occasion, he had made plans to go out with his two best friends, but each time, his plans fell through. They had to go on without him while he banged away at his computer, completing motions and briefing cases.

This week, his workload was a bit on the light side, so it wasn't his schedule that was keeping him from agreeing to Chalie's suggestion; it was his meager access to cash. He knew he was practically broke. If he did decide to go, Thomas and Chalie would definitely have to pay the tip.

"Okay," Ben finally said. "I'll go."

"You better not be lying, man."

"Didn't I say that I was coming?"

Chalie used his cross examination voice. "How many times have you said you were coming and you ended up a no-show?"

"Okay, okay," Ben said, laughing into the phone. "Stop breathing on a brother like a dragon. I promise I'll come this time. If I don't, I'll foot the bill for your wedding."

This time, Chalie laughed into the phone. "If you had any idea how much it's going to cost, you wouldn't say that, even as a joke."

"Are you sure you're ready to tie the knot?" Ben asked, noting the despair in his friend's voice.

"No doubt. It's the best decision I've ever made," Chalie said, sounding giddy. "Look, let me get back to work and I'll see you at five forty-five sharp. If you're a no-show, I hope you're sitting on a bank, my dude." Chalie ended the call.

Ben dropped the phone on his desk and sat for a minute in contemplative silence. Yeah, Gina must have thrown some really good stuff on Chalie, because it was obvious that he was deeply in love with her. Back in law school, Chalie had been the pickiest bachelor Ben had ever seen. It seemed that every single female who came at Chalie was either 'too this' or 'too that.' He didn't think Chalie would ever find someone he would adore like Gina. But Chalie was a good man, and he deserved to have someone like Gina in his life.

As Ben thought about Chalie and Gina, he brought up the home screen on his iPhone and strolled through the text messages that he and Dana had been sending each other ever since they'd met, not even a full week ago. He recalled her soft caramel colored skin and the way she kept her hair pulled back so that he could see all of that beautiful face. To Ben she was simply fine.

Ben had always considered himself an average-looking guy. He thought that he had a nice build with some attractive features, but not the kind of looks that made women do double-takes. But when he met her at Rick's she had done a double-take on him and then actually approached him, starting up a conversation.

He would be lying if he said that they didn't click immediately. The connection between them was undeniable and just the thought of her gave him butterflies. When they talked, they spoke with ease as though they'd

known each other for years instead of just
days. And when they did have sex, which was a
bit too quick for him if he was being honest
about it, it was explosive. Their bodies had
meshed together as though God had handcrafted
them solely for each other. Together, they
seemed perfect. But there was one slight
issue keeping them from having a happily-
ever-after.

Dana was married.

* * *

Ben continued to bang away at his
computer keyboard as the day turned to
evening, slowly reigning in the official start
of the weekend when his cell phone buzzed.
It was a text from Dana which read: *Hey, Mr.
Bains.*

Ben smiled and typed out a response as
fast as he could: *Hey babe.*

The words: *Whatcha doing?* appeared on his
screen.

*Working,* he responded.

She texted that she missed Ben and that
she had a really good time with him on
Tuesday evening. She then asked Ben if he
was going to be busy this evening, when Ben
responded that he had dinner tonight with two
friends at Rick's.

Dana responded: *Can we meet after? I miss
u baby.*

Ben: *Sure babe. How 'bout 8?*

Dana: *K.*

Ben: *My place? Incognito?*

Dana: *K. See you then. xoxoxoxo*

* * *

Ben arrived at Rick's restaurant right around 5:45 p.m. Chalie and Thomas arrived shortly thereafter. The time they spent together in law school felt like they had gone to war together and that is what had, and would bind them together for all time.

During their law school years they enjoyed many memorable moments that would in time, become stories. This dinner, in its simplest terms, served as a time to retell those old stories, and tell new stories that had developed since they last spoke to each other.

Ben asked Thomas, "Do you remember that time during our first semester when we stayed up all night studying for that Con Law exam, and I didn't understand anything and——"

Thomas cut in, "I spent all night explaining it to you, and the same stuff I was explaining to you was on the exam. Somehow you got a better grade than me."

"Yeah! That was funny!"

"It wasn't funny to me," Thomas harped. "You knowledge thief."

They laughed.

"No, Thomas," Chalie said, "the best was the time that you hadn't read a case and got called on in class to brief it, and like, you're making up the answer while me and Ben are making up flash cards for you to read and passing them to you."

"That was hilarious," Ben exclaimed.

"Yeah, so like, Ben and I are handing the cards with the answers on them while professor Tass was putting you on blast asking all kinds of crazy questions."

"He had to have known I didn't read the case, but he couldn't get me to answer wrong. I know he was pissed," Thomas said.

By now they were laughing so hard it hurt.

And they continued to tell stories of old as they ordered and ate their dinner.

Eventually they moved from the past to the present as Thomas told his latest story. He told of his new bride and how they recently learned that they were pregnant. He simply could not wait for their first child. Chalie told of his pleasure with his long time girlfriend, now fiancée, Gina. Both Thomas and Chalie spoke of stability and the good life, as both were working in well established law firms.

Ben told a different story, for his life had taken quite a different course. He told them of his clerkship duties and recent encounter with Dana. He told of the excitement and how, for some reason she seemed to stay on his mind.

Chalie, grinning through half sarcastic teeth, asked, "Dude, when are you ever gonna settle down?"

Thomas chimed in, "I always wondered how you kept all them women at arm's length. I still wonder."

"You know what? I think I kind of like her," Ben admitted.

Laughter roared from both Chalie and Thomas.

"What's so funny?"

"This is the one you like?" Chalie roared as he took a bite of his Porterhouse.

Thomas added his impressions, "You think you like the married mystery girl. Man, I tell you." He chuckled. "You still add flavor to my otherwise boring life."

Dinner did eventually wind down and sometime around 7:15 they ended their rendezvous. Ben had to put his share of the tab on his credit card. As he watched the waiter take his credit card to run it, he almost fell ill over the prospect of it being declined and then having to face the embarrassment in front of his friends. His relief was overwhelming when the waiter approached Ben with the receipt for him to sign. Had it been a few days later Ben was certain that the card would not have gone through.

After they said their goodbyes Ben went to relieve himself in the restroom. As he relieved himself, his mind wandered off to Dana. He envisioned her soft skin and full ripe lips. Her legs, long and slender. Her smooth as velvet voice. He closed his eyes in sweet memory. The image was so strong he could smell the allure of her perfume. It made him feel good all over, and his heart began to hammer. Eight o'clock just could not come fast enough for him.

While washing his hands, Ben looked up into the mirror. Behind his own image in the mirror, he saw furtive movement startling him and bringing him out of his trance.

In the reflection he saw a tall black baldheaded man leaning on a wall by the door. Ben had been so engrossed in thought about Dana that he hadn't heard him enter.

The bald man held a briefcase in his

hand and wore black, thick rimmed glasses. Through the reflection, the bald man stared directly into Ben's eyes. With a sharp voice that reeked of confidence, he said, "Ben, I need your help."

# CHAPTER FOUR

Ben's eyes narrowed with suspicion as he turned off the water. Drying his hands, he threw a slow appraising glance at the bald man. *What the hell is this guy's deal,* he thought.

Ben asked, "Do I know you?"

"No, no," he replied with a bashful smile. He bent over in pseudo-embarrassment. "I'm sorry. My name is Darren Hall."

"Okay—Darren Hall?" Ben squinted his eyes. "What's up? How do you know my name?" Ben started thinking that maybe it was time to get out of the bathroom.

Confident, like he was speaking to a longtime friend, he said, "Listen, Ben, I can explain everything but, it's really sensitive stuff." Darren Hall looked over his shoulder as if to check and see if the coast was clear. "Why don't we go outside and talk, where, you know, we can speak more freely?"

Ben's eyes shifted and his face tightened. "I don't think so." He began to forge his way to the door.

Before Ben could get past him, Darren opened the brief case. As if appealing to Ben's subconscious mind, he whispered, "Look here."

Ben looked down into the opened briefcase and saw that it was loaded with neatly packed bundles of $100 bills. His stomach became tight and palms clammy. With saucer-sized eyes, he gazed down at the cash and froze.

Darren Hall rested his hand on the money. "This is twenty-five thousand dollars. This—is also what I need to talk to you about."

A stress line formed on Ben's brow. His first instinct, driven by common sense, was to leave the bathroom, post haste. His second instinct, driven by curiosity and greed, told him to hear Darren out.

His eyes darted back forth. He couldn't make head nor tails of the situation, and it presented a bit more temptation than Ben felt he could withstand. In a month he'd be unemployed, and soon he would default on his student loans amongst other financial obligations he had.

"Listen, if I go outside with you, it has to be where we can be seen." Ben didn't trust this guy any farther than he could throw him. If he tried something funny, Ben wanted to be where he could yell to passersby for help to get the police.

"How about where we can be seen, but not where people can hear our conversation?"

"Fair enough."

Across the street they found a bench facing Ocean Drive next to the beach.

Ben had one foot propped up on the bench. Curious as to how this man knew who he was, Ben asked, "How do you know my name?"

"You're the law clerk to Judge Pomerance."

"Yeah, but how do *you* know that?"

"It's public information. I saw it on the courthouse website," Darren Hall answered in a matter-of-fact tone.

*He does have a point,* Ben thought. He changed his demeanor to a lesser degree of defensiveness. "So then, Darren Hall, what's this all about?"

"Listen," Darren began as he leaned back. "I know you feel as though you're taking a risk by coming out here to talk to me, so I'm going to give it to you straight and simple." He looked at Ben in all sincerity. "I'm a minority stockholder in a corporation called Overton Industries. I own maybe $250,000 of stock and maybe that equates to me owning one-sixteenth of one percent of all of Overton Industries' stock.

"There's this guy, Walt Killinger, who is a majority stockholder of Overton Industries. He owns 51% of Overton's stock, besides being the CEO and Chairman of the Board."

Walt Killinger. Ben knew the name well. Ben also knew the case. He wondered where he was going with this.

Darren continued, "I have reason to believe he's stealing from the little stockholders, like myself. Well, maybe not stealing, but lying about the value of our stock.

"The rumor, which seems to be quite viable, is that he orchestrated the purchase of some eight subsidiaries by Overton. I believe that these subsidiaries have technology that can turn sea water into potable water at one tenth the current cost."

Darren's eyes intensified. "A huge, huge, invention. But, the problem is that he hasn't told anyone about it." He thought Ben should have figured it all out by now.

Ben held a blank face.

He continued, "So, that means my stock is undervalued. See, if he did buy these subsidiaries and they hold the technology I think they do, my $250,000 of stock would be worth at least 2.5 million. See, just the *mere news* of the acquisition of these eight subsidiaries would send the value of the stock through the roof.

"So, Ben, as you can see why, as far as I'm concerned, he is stealing well over two million of my hard earned money. Do you know how long it took me to earn that $250,000 to invest? I worked hard to save and earn that money, and now this asshole is going to jerk me around like this? I can't allow it."

Ben looked on, like, where exactly do I fit in? "Why don't you file a derivative suit?"

"I would. Believe me, I would. You don't know how badly I want to do that. But, the problem is, I just can't go file a law suit against this guy without some type of proof to start off with. I'd get sued for filing a frivolous lawsuit. He and his army of lawyers would kill me. What I need is some proof that he, through Overton, actually bought those subsidiaries, and, that they possess that water invention. That's where you come in."

"How?"

"Well, I know that Killinger is currently engaged in a divorce battle. And

I know that 92 boxes of 'secret files' are stored in Judge Pomerance's evidence room."

Ben now knew for sure what Darren Hall wanted him to do. He backed up a bit and said, "That's under seal, by order of the Court. I can't go in there. Do you know what kind of trouble I would get into if I went in there?" He sure did.

"Ben, you haven't heard me out yet. Listen. I'm not asking you to do anything I thought would land you in any trouble. Think about it, if you get caught, I'd get caught, and I don't want that to happen. All I want is my rights as a stockholder honored. To start the process of having my rights, and the rights of every other minority stockholder honored is, to find out if there is an inter-board memo in there regarding one of the eight subsidiaries, and some proof of it. That is all I need to know in order to file my lawsuit."

Ben thought for a moment before answering. "Let me get this straight. You want me to break into Judge Pomerance's evidence room, look through the Killinger files which have been sealed by Court order, illegally fiddle around until I find one of eight memos, if they do exist. And if they do exist and I find one, make a copy and give it to you?"

"Yes. That's it. The entire deal."

"And I get $25,000?"

"Every single solitary dime."

"And then you file a derivative suit?"

"That's right. Exactly. Of course, I would never mention your name. That would not be in either of our best interests."

Ben couldn't believe it was that simple. There had to be a catch. "That's it?"

"That's it," he repeated as he patted his hand on the briefcase, "and the $25,000 is all yours."

Ben stood there weighing his options.

The whole time while he thought, Darren Hall never took his eyes off of Ben.

Ben just couldn't make up his mind right then, right there. He had too many thoughts to sort through. Two thoughts actually: one side consisted of $25,000 and the other side consisted of jail and disbarment. He couldn't think straight. He needed time.

Ben finally answered, "I have to think about it."

"Well, don't think too long. I need an answer soon or the deal is off. Time is money. I'll give you until, say, Monday evening. I'll be here at…" Darren Hall looked at his watch, "…ten p.m. All right? If you're here with a memo, I'll know we have a deal."

Ben thought for an extra moment or two. He figured he didn't have to show up. In fact, right then he decided for sure that he would not. But to appease him, Ben said, "Okay."

Before Darren left, with the sincerity of a priest he said, "Ben, we—the minority stockholders, need your help." Then he disappeared into the darkness of the beach.

With the shock still wearing on him, Ben thought, *this feels surreal.* He sat on the bench for a while as Darren's words echoed back and forth in his mind. He had told himself that there would be no way he would do what Darren Hall had asked of him. But just for shits and giggles, he pondered the idea.

    *It would be a simple task,* he thought, and then he would get $25,000 in cold hard cash. Twenty-five thousand dollars that he really needed. All for one little innocent photocopy of a memo. Something that a stockholder has a right to know anyway. *Maybe I could,* he thought. *It won't hurt anybody. It would be like a victimless crime.*

    Knowing that no decision would come quickly, he figured that he had all weekend to think about Darren Hall and Overton Industries. He had more pressing things to do, like go home and get ready for Dana. He lived two blocks away and walked home. On the way he picked up a bottle of chardonnay.

* * *

    When he arrived at his apartment building he put on a weathered pair of jeans and a T-shirt, his favorite outfit in the whole wide world. He went into the kitchen where he found himself a cork screw, opened the bottle of wine and poured himself a glass. He went out on the porch steps of the apartment building and kicked his feet up on the railing and began to wait. The proper name of this activity, he thought, is known as chilling out. It had been quite some time since he had just sat and did absolutely, completely nothing. And it felt good.

    Even though Ben worked long hours, he never complained. No one had ever given Ben a thing in his life. To make it as an attorney he had worked extremely hard and had been rather strict on himself. The hard work had

42

gotten him through college and law school.
Right after law school he landed a job with
Judge Pomerance as his law clerk.

As a result of pushing himself so hard
over the past eight years, at age twenty-six
he had started to feel worn down. As of late,
he had to begin to think that maybe he needed
a break from all the monotony. This weekend
would allow him to rest and enjoy himself as
he considered that the $25,000 would buy him
a much needed vacation.

He laid his head back and enjoyed the
Miami night air. He found inner-solace in the
fact that the ocean was only two blocks away
from where he sat. He loved the whole idea of
living so close to the beach. He smiled to
himself.

When he looked up, much to his delight,
he saw Dana approaching from the end of the
block. Upon her sight he began to fidget.
Although a block away he could tell it was
her. He could see the outline of the body
he had held so tight in so many places only
three nights ago.

Before he knew it she was right there
at the porch where he sat. Bending down and
smiling she French-kissed him. Ben lost
all concept of time and space. His world
consisted solely of her tongue and his mouth.
Nothing else. She grabbed his face and laced
it with kisses, charging him beyond belief.

As she straddled him in his chair, her
purse fell to floor, knocking over his glass
of wine.

She whispered in his ear, "I had a
really good time Tuesday night."

"Me too," Ben confessed.

"And, I wanted to thank you for all of the legal advice."

Ben shrugged it off. "It's nothing."

"Actually, it's a lot. You have no idea."

Ben smiled. "I've got some wine upstairs. Do you want some?"

While rubbing her hand on his crotch, she answered, "I do."

Ben tilted his head towards the door. "Come on."

Upstairs, Ben handed Dana a glass of wine. They retreated to the bedroom, where, for the next hour and a half they had sex with the intensity of a bull fight.

After all that energy had been released, they cuddled for a while, then enjoyed pizza and the rest of the wine on Ben's balcony.

Dana inquired, "So, Mr. Esquire, tell me your story."

"What story?"

"You know, how did this beautiful man sitting next to me end up a lawyer in Miami, Florida?" She rubbed the back of his hand.

Ben looked out across South Beach's art deco architectural genre. After a long pause, he replied, "I know nothing about you. I don't even know your last name."

"Selvey. There, now you know."

"Well, I guess that answers it all for me."

"What?"

"You know where I work, where I live, my last name—I know very little about you. How about we keep it real and you give me some information on you first?"

She continued to rub the back of his hand at the same gentle pace she had before he answered. As her eyes grew heavy she looked down. Ben waited for the answer.

"That's true, I know more about you," she replied. "You want me to keep it real but, what we have between us, whatever it is, isn't exactly real."

"Damn," he said, looking introspective.

"What?"

"That makes me feel cheap."

"Cheap?"

"Yes, cheap. You know about me. What do I know about you? Cheap is what I feel like."

"Don't feel that way. I like spending time with you. I mean," she softened her voice, "I'm here. If you just give me some time, I promise, I'll tell you everything you want to know about me." She shook her head. "I just can't do it right now, but I swear I will, soon. I promise."

If this were Texas Hold'Em, Ben would have folded two cards before the flop with a pair of Jacks in his hand. He was like mush in her hands and he gave in. Ben responded, "Okay, what do you want to know?"

She smiled. "Do you have any family?"

"Not living. My dad died when I was in the ninth grade."

Her face cringed. "That must've been awful."

"It was. He was everything to me."

"What about your mom?"

"She was extremely irresponsible. I think I raised her after my dad died." He seemed to have resentment in his voice.

"When did she pass?"

"In 2002. She died from a stroke."

"That's awful."

"It was." Ben took a bite off of his pizza crust.

"Siblings?"

"One sister. Twin sister, in fact."

"Really? How did she pass?"

Ben leaned back and rocked in his chair for a pensive moment before he began. "She had a way about her where people were just drawn to her.

"At the time she had this boyfriend, for about five years. It had gotten to the point where she just couldn't handle him anymore. I mean, she couldn't go to the grocery store without having him follow her to make sure she wasn't cheating on him.

"He would constantly call her job, and she would lose job after job because of this guy. He was rude, overbearing, fiercely jealous, and over protective.

"Finally, she tells him, 'I don't want you anymore,' and he wasn't having it. So, on New Year's Eve, she's getting out of the shower, getting ready to go to a church service, and he broke into her apartment. His theory on things was that either he was going to have her, or no one was going to have her. And he meant it.

"As she got out of the shower, he shot her six times at point blank range. He went into the kitchen and called the police and waited for them to arrive. He did it because he said he couldn't live without her."

"That's horrible."

"Tell me about it."

"What happened to the boyfriend?"

"He got 25 years to life, not that it makes me feel any better. I went to therapy for a year because of that. I think about her every day. And that was it—that left me all by myself."

"Did the therapy help?"

"The therapist says it did."

She looked at Ben sideways. "You feel like you're by yourself in the world now that your sister is gone, don't you?"

Ben didn't answer.

"I feel alone, too, Ben, and I'm not trying to hide it." She leaned in and kissed him. Eventually, Ben took her hand and led her back to the bedroom where they made love again.

Afterward, laying in bed both naked and physically satisfied, they engaged in conversation for an easy hour and coalesced. Both the enjoyment and length of the conversation happened upon them unexpectedly.

Time had flown by and Dana checked her cell phone which read 11:32 p.m.

"Oh my," she gasped. "Big Ben," she leaned in and kissed him, "I've gotta go. He's going to start wondering soon."

"He?" Ben said.

"My husband."

"I know. Are you sure he's going to *start wondering*? Like, he hasn't been wondering since eight o'clock?"

"Trust me." She grabbed her belongings and rushed off to the shower. Ten minutes later, fully dressed, she emerged from the bathroom.

Ben implored, "When can I see you again? You know how I feel alone in this world."

She smiled. "As soon as I can get away. I promise." She bent over and kissed him again. "I swear I'll be thinking of you every moment. If I can't see you, or text you, believe me, you'll be on my mind."

And with that, she was gone.

Ten minutes after she left, Ben couldn't help himself so he texted her, asking her if she missed him yet. She quickly replied, "Of course, silly." The texts continued between them:

Ben: *I didn't expect to enjoy the conversation that much.*

Dana: *Me either. I enjoyed it almost as much as the xoxo.*

Ben: *I think I'm addicted to you.*

Dana: *:)*

Ben: *I'm going through withdrawal.*

Dana: *U sound like a stalker. LOL.*

Ben: *Can't be. Don't know where you live.*

Dana: *You haven't tried hard enough ;)*

Ben: *You're not texting and driving, r u?*

Dana: *Not driving. In a cab.*

Ben: *So then, you do live close by?*

Dana: *Cut it out, Matlock. :) I'm almost home, gotta go now.*

Ben: *Babe, text me tomorrow?*

Dana: *Count on it.*

"*Good name in man or woman, dear my Lord is the immediate jewel of their souls: who steals my purse steals trash; 'tis something, nothings, 'twas mine, 'tis his, and has been slave to thousands. But he that filches from me my good name robs me of that which not enriches him, and makes me poor indeed.*"

~William Shakespeare

# CHAPTER FIVE

Sunday. Day 7.
August 8, 2010

When Rawlings saw Tommy he immediately knew something was up. Rawlings spouted at Tommy, "What gives? Someting wrong? I just had a good renewal visit, to come back 'ere, and see you standin' 'ere in my livin' room. I know dat mean someting wrong."

Rawlings had just returned from the Cayman Islands and Columbia, a trip that he had taken with his daughter, Mariah. Rawlings had couched it to his daughter and her mother as a vacation to South America where he could spend time with his daughter and visit old friends. Mariah's mother, Daria, knew that Rawlings was telling a half truth, but it didn't matter to her. She knew what Rawlings was and she knew that come hell or high water, Rawlings would protect Mariah. Mariah was just happy to spend time with her dad.

Tuesday morning around 6:30 a.m. they flew out of Miami International Airport and arrived at Owen Roberts International Airport in Grand Caymen about an hour later. After checking into their hotel room Rawlings made his rounds and deposited roughly $720,000 in cash into three separate offshore accounts. Then, he enjoyed himself the rest of the day playing cricket at the Royal Palms Hotel and Cricket Grounds. Mariah watched him play for the first three hours then spent the rest of her daylight hours reading a book and drinking virgin daiquiris at the resort pool.

That night Rawlings and Mariah enjoyed a five star dinner, compliments of the president of the Bank of the Grand Cay. It was quite the dining the experience with more waiters attending to their needs than a colony of ants. It made Mariah feel like a queen and that pleased Rawlings. The Bank of the Grand Cay appreciated Rawlings's business, which Rawlings clearly understood by the sheer grandeur and pomp of the dinner. The dinner between Rawlings and Mariah had been going off without a hitch, when he gave her a gift, which she simply adored.

Sitting across the table from Rawlings his daughter gazed into his eyes. "Thank you, Daddy," she exclaimed. "This is one of the nicest gifts ever."

Fifteen years old, clever, and with a smile that could melt stone into lava, she had been raised to be and was, a princess. Her mother made sure that her grades were good enough for her to get into some of the best private schools in the Metro-Dade area. Her father made sure that he could afford it. Even though her mother and father had never lived together, they worked closely with each other through the years to bring her up in the best environment they could.

Rawlings watched her beam and not being able to hold it in, a smile emerged on his face like sunshine breaking through the clouds.

The 10-carat Tiffany diamond necklace was one of the most beautiful sights her eyes had ever seen. The bling from the diamond was blinding. She held it tenderly in her hands, with care, like one would hold a newborn kitten. Not able to contain herself she stood and walked around the table to give him a tense hug which she held longer than usual. Sensing her unease Rawlings pulled away from her to get a look at her face, scanning it to see if he could get any indication as to what was on her mind.

Ignoring the inquisitive gaze of her father she sat back down, setting her folded hands on the table.

A bus boy approached and began clearing the table while another filled Mariah and Rawlings's glasses with water for the tenth time. A waiter appeared from the opposite side of the table asking, "Will you two be having any dessert this evening?"

"No tank yuh," Rawlings responded and the waiter left.

Nothing was said between Rawlings and Mariah until their water glasses were topped off and the bus boy had finished clearing the table, scurrying off into the kitchen area.

"Baby girl, now wat eats at de heart of ya?"

"Daddy, I think I want to come work with you. I think it'd be fun." Like her mother she had skin the color of hazelnut and her eyes were dark as sapphire, like her father.

"Yuh goin' ta college, no? I tout yuh want to teach 'bout histree?"

"I've had a change of heart. I want to work for you. Work with you."

Saying 'no' to her had always been difficult to Rawlings. In fact, he could count the number of times he had actually told her 'no' in her whole life. In the moment as he sat there, staring into the eyes of all that he held dear, he determined that so long as destiny, fate or the gods that be would allow it, he would withhold a 'yes' from her all of his might, while still refusing to say 'no.'

"Git yuh degree first, chile. Den we talk 'bout cha workin' wit me. De college educated mind, dats wat me need for help."

She reeled back and asked, "Why not now? Do you think I can't handle it?"

"Baby girl, it's not 'bout handlin'. It be hard, grindin' work. Wear yuh down from the soul out to da body."

"Daddy, what exactly do you do? What kind of business can be that hard?"

At this point Rawlings understood this was a question of rhetoric. "Dis yuh know—me a *bizness* man. Why yuh ask?"

"You say you're a business man. I'm pretty sure I know what your business is. How could I not? I hear things and see things, Daddy."

Today was a day Rawlings was sure would come, bringing a degree of sadness to him. He knew he was a man whose reputation tended to precede him and with Mariah being as smart as she was, he knew eventually she would figure things out. But he still didn't like the idea of his little girl knowing what he did for a living, and he was feeling rather uncomfortable at the moment.

His heart denied his brain's almost
unrelenting request to allow his lip to
twitch. He reminded himself that this was his
daughter and that he had to remain calm. She
would not take too kindly to the outburst
thing.

Blandly he responded, "What chu 'ere
now, girl?"

"I hear you are a very respected man
and that when people make you angry, you
do things to make them *really* regret it."
Before Rawlings could respond she checked
the immediate area around them to make sure
no one could hear her and then leaned in her
father's direction. She asked as though she
had been waiting years to know the answer
and if she didn't ask soon, she was going to
burst, "Do you kill people, Daddy? Just tell
me the truth, I can handle it."

Stunned at the directness of her
question Rawlings leaned back in his seat.
Secretly, he was proud of his daughter,
coming out with her question so direct and
unwavering.

He responded, "I thought ya said yuh
knew what me do for a livin'?"

"I do know, okay, Daddy? And my point is
this——you won't let me work for you because
it's dangerous. Because I might get hurt. But
that's exactly why I want *you* to stop."

Interestingly enough he thought that's
why he had let Demetrius into his inner
circle, so he wouldn't have to deal anymore.
But when Demetrius failed, Rawlings had
to come to grips with the fact that he
actually enjoyed the art of what he did
for a living. Rawlings knew he had talent

and all the special skills needed to be a successful drug kingpin. If he were to leave the drug business now, he felt that it would be the equivalent of Michael Jordan's first retirement from the NBA. A waste of talent. He really enjoyed what he did and quitting now, he realized, would be harder than just *quitting*.

Having nothing but an awkward wall of silence between them Mariah gingerly placed her hand on her father's and asked, "Do you remember that time when I was a little girl I stayed at your house and there was a butterfly in my room? I wanted you to kill it. I was so scared of it. But you said, 'No, this here butterfly, it's beautiful.'

"You said it represented life. You chased that thing around the house for at least a half hour, and when you caught it, you cupped it gently in your hands. You had me open the door, and you took it outside. I watched you let it go free. Do you remember that?"

"I do," he said with ease.

She looked confused. "Am I missing something? That's the person I know, but I keep hearing some disheartening stories about you."

Rawlings picked up his cup of ice water and took a sip. He set the glass down and smiled a little smile at her, as he said, "When me was da age of yuh, me was poor. I connive me way ta dis country from Jamaica." His voice was soft and gentle. "Me get here, den work hard as a janitor in de hospital, doin' da nightshift for extra pay. Me say den, my chile no gon grow up poor an

strugglin'. Me hustle and claw me way outta
poorer than a pauper. Now, me provide plenty
for yuh and yuh mudda. She a good woman. We
bofe do best we can by yuh."

With easiness in her young voice she
replied, "They say karma is everything. Do
you, you know, ever regret what you do? Like
karma may come back to get you? Take you away
from me?"

He paused again as he gathered his
thoughts, then said, "Everyting me do, every
bizness move me make, know dat me have
respected de life and respect de beauty in
all dat me see. Me never have, and me never
will take eida life or beauty without de just
cause. Whatcha tink happen to dat butterfly
if me tink him hurt you? Me smash him on
the wall—flat. Me no change from when you
a little girl. Me da same man who let dat
butterfly go."

"Smashing butterflies or not, I'd feel a
lot safer if you would change your line of
work. Money isn't everything, Daddy."

He stared at the table as he thought. "I
know, but yuh ask a lot."

"Can you at least think about it?"

"I will."

She twisted her face and tilted her
head. "Do you promise?"

"I promise, baby girl."

"Okay, Daddy. But you know I love you no
matter what. I just want you to be safe, like
you want me to be safe."

"Me know, baby girl. Me know."

The rest of the evening was restful
and relaxing as it could have been under
the circumstances for the two of them, as

neither he nor Mariah made reference to that
conversation for the rest of the trip.

The next day, on Wednesday, they flew
to Columbia. The purpose of this leg of
his 'vacation' was to meet with some of
his suppliers and renew friendships he had
originally forged in the mid-90s. Every once
in a while, Rawlings wanted to show his face
to his Latin friends. He thought it was good
business etiquette.

He was always on time, never haggled
about price, and paid on time. All the
Colombians liked him. But of all the
Colombians, he was liked the most by Raul
Palta. Raul and Rawlings were almost like
family now. Raul's daughter was the same age
as Rawlings's daughter. So while they talked
business, the kids were free to roam and ride
horseback on Raul's 46,000 acre ranch outside
of Medellín.

He stayed there until Sunday afternoon,
when he and Mariah caught a flight out of
Medellín. They did not make it back into
Miami until 10:00 p.m. He dropped his
daughter off at her mother's home.

When he arrived at home, he was tired
and in a crotchety mood. The fact that
Tommy was waiting for him in his living
room when he arrived home did not help lift
his spirits. Tommy's presence at this hour
usually meant that something had gone wrong.

Rawlings waved his hands, beckoning the
news to be told. "Lehme 'ere de bad news,
mon. Just git it out, now."

Tommy hesitated.

"Tommy, wat? It's tat bad yuh nah can
tell me? Huh? Wat happen? Did some bwoy git

me daughter pregnant?" He said it tongue-in-cheek as he looked at Tommy while he sat down and took off his shoes. To Rawlings nothing could be worse than Mariah getting knocked up, and he was sure Tommy, as usual, was going to tell him of some small time issue that had arisen while he was gone.

"No, it's worse," Tommy said softly.

"Tommy, no ting worse den me daughter getting' pregnant 'fore she married. Yuh got dat?" Tensely he said, "Now tell me."

Tommy gave it to him. "Someone stole our Liberty City receipts Wednesday morning."

Rawlings hit the ceiling. His dreadlocks bounced around like rag doll hair as he jumped to his feet. "Someone stole wat?" He put his hand to his ear. "I nah quite 'ere you, mon. Ya say someone stole our Liberty City receipts?"

Tommy dared not answer, but his silence was answer enough. Rawlings yelled as he picked up the lamp on the table next to him and hurled it at a section of the glass wall that looked out into the Atlantic Ocean. The glass shattered as the lamp and glass collided making a thunderclap. Tommy flinched at the sound.

Rawlings stormed around the room like a little gremlin, rubbing his chin. "Who waz it, Tommy?"

"I don't know. But the streets are trying to find out who did this."

"Good. Fuckin' good. Put dis out on da street too." He turned and pointed at Tommy. "Tell whoever can tell me who stole me money will git a reward. Personally. From me. Fifty tousand...no, one hundred. One hundred tousand dollars for da name. You got dat, Tommy? One hundred tousand dollars."

Rawlings could have just as easily offered two hundred thousand dollars as a reward. He didn't care. His reputation is what was stolen from him and as far as he was concerned its value could never be assessed in tangible monetary terms. One couldn't buy a reputation like Rawlings had, even if one were as rich as Bill Gates. Either you had it, or you didn't.

Rawlings, wise as he was, fully understood that his most tried and true associates couldn't always be on the street, watching every transaction, monitoring every sale.

He knew that his reputation could be there, doing more than the eyes and ears of an associate. His reputation could be more pervasive in the midst of the minds and thoughts of every friend and enemy alike, all the time, influencing every presumption, conclusion, and imagination.

His reputation meant power and control, and that agent of power and control had been squarely placed in jeopardy by some brazen act of disrespect. As of now, as a business issue, preservation of his reputation was his primary concern and this issue had to be dealt with swiftly and sternly, no matter what the cost.

Like a troll he continued to pace around the room. "And when I find out who it is and git me hands on him...ohhh, dey gon wish dey never been born. I swear." He stopped and looked at Tommy. "How much did dey get?"

Tommy hesitated again. "It was a

THE LAW CLERK

particularly good week, Raw."

"Dammit, Tommy, I ask yuh a simple
question. An idiot can answer da damn
question. I no ask how da fuckin' week was, I
ask yuh how much money did dey git."

"About two hundred grand."

Rawlings picked up another lamp and
threw it through another section of the glass
wall. That shattered also. "Dammit it all! It
is worse dan me daughter gettin' pregnant,"
he yelled. "Listen to me, Tommy." He balled
his fists up as he talked. "I wan everybody,
and I mean everybody on da payroll lookin' an
listenin' for who did tis. Are yuh listenin'?
'Cause we need to git dese guys whoever dey
are. I mean, even da police on da payroll.
Dis is our top priority and I wan ya on dis
one personally. We cannot afford to let dis
slip. Our reputation is on de line. Yuh got
dat?"

Tommy did not know if he was to answer.

"Tommy, yuh got dat?"

"Yeah, Raw. I got it."

"Good. Git on it, den." Rawlings grabbed
his shoes and headed upstairs to sulk.
Before he went up the stairs, he turned and
said, "And call someone to come fix me damn
windows—fuck!" Then he turned around and
stormed up the stairs and disappeared.

* * *

Ben woke up and reached for his cell
phone and checked to see if Dana had texted
him. He found, to his dismay that she
hadn't. He tried to text Dana, but his phone
displayed an error message.

"Damn," he exclaimed, dropping his head down. "They turned off my phone." Last week he had made a strategic decision to pay his electric bill and then wait until the very last moment, which was yesterday, to pay his cell phone bill. Only he had forgotten to pay the bill.

The only call the phone would allow was to his cell phone carrier, so he called and tried to talk them into turning the phone back on immediately. He went online and paid the minimum due to have his service restored, but they advised that the soonest his phone could be turned on was late Monday. It had something to do with their re-activation policy.

With no cell phone and no access to Dana, Ben spent the remainder of his weekend playing beach volleyball during the day and watching manly movies on TNT, all the while contemplating Darren Hall's offer and thinking of Dana.

Monday morning. Day 8.
August 9, 2010

Monday morning arrived and all the sun and fun of the weekend was gone. The time read 8:28 a.m. and the line to get into the courthouse seemed longer than ever. Each and every person who entered the courthouse had to be checked for contraband. Even the line to the right reserved for courthouse employees was longer than usual today.

It looked like an airport. Everybody, every bag, every cup of coffee was checked for contraband. Ben marveled at the analogy that materialized in his mind: access to justice could take a long time.

When Ben finally reached the front of the line, a large woolly-faced officer with a bushy mustache parted his lips and teeth shone from under the mound of hair on his upper lip. He smiled. "Ben," he said. "Mornin'."

"Morning, Butch," Ben answered. "How was your weekend?"

"It was good until Sunday night, because I knew I had to be here in the morning. But it's good to have a weekend off every now and then."

"Tell me about it," Ben replied with a sigh.

Butch grinned as he went through Ben's bag. Once he was satisfied that Ben was not armed, Ben went through the magnetometer without incident.

Ben scuttled down the hall to the elevators. A crowd of litigants and lawyers had gathered there. Like a pack of lions, they waited for the next elevator as if it were prey. Ben didn't wait and took the stairs to the fifth floor.

At 8:42 a.m., he arrived at an open door
which read: Judge Pomerance.

Alyse, the judge's secretary sat at
her desk in the foyer. She was much more
than just the judge's secretary to Ben. Ben
considered her to be a friend. He gave her a
warm greeting.

Opening the morning mail, she replied,
"Hello."

On her desk sat a steaming hot cup of
tea with milk in it. Alyse, always as a rule,
had at least one piping hot cup of tea in the
morning and one in the afternoon. She had
'Rules of Thumb' when it came to tea. Rule
number one was that the tea must be "piping"
hot. Warm or hot just would not suffice,
Alyse would always say. Rule number two: tea
without milk is simply uncivilized.

Ben eased by her desk, and she
nonchalantly muttered, "The student loan
people called again."

"What did they want?" He feigned
surprise.

Sarcastically, she answered, "They
wanted to thank you for paying off your
student loan thirty years early."

"Very funny." He knew good and well
what they had called about. They had called
to harass Ben about being delinquent in his
repayment. "What did you tell them?"

"Oh, I told them that if they called
back again, they would be sued for calling
your place of employment after being told not
to under the Fair Debt Collections Practices
Act."

Ben wondered how she knew that law, but
did not ask. "Thanks, Alyse," he said as he

shuffled into his office.

He sat down and looked in dismay at the mass of papers on his desk. Three stack of papers that looked like mountains.

A new week meant a new set of motion papers. It meant a new set of cases and a new set of facts for which Ben must research and find applicable law. Each stack stood approximately two feet high and it meant that long hours awaited his utmost attention.

Next to each pile were the judge's notes to Ben. The judge had read each and every paper in the stack and written a note as to how he wanted each motion to be decided.

That was how the judge spent his weekends—reading motion papers at home. He was a workaholic, and Ben sometimes despised him for it. Responsibility for writing the details and the opinion that resolves the issues in the motion papers or "the papers" as the judge referred to them, fell on Ben.

In acceptance of the fact that the weekend was now officially over, he took a deep breath and began to un-stack the papers. First, he counted them in order to see how many opinions he would have to write. One opinion for each set of motion papers. A set of motion papers consisted of a "notice of motion" by the moving party and a "notice of cross motion" or an "answer" by the non-moving party. When he had counted them all, he sighed.

Forty-nine motions.

The thought made his heart sick. He had never done forty-nine motions in one week. He knew this week would indeed be the longest of his young legal career.

# THE LAW CLERK

He placed the stack of papers on the shelves behind him and grabbed the first two papers off the top. He took a deep breath, and with all the concentration he could muster, began to read them.

# CHAPTER SIX
Monday afternoon. Day 8.
August 9, 2010


J.C sat in the back of Mr. G's watching the
soap operas as he did with religious fervor
every day. Everybody who worked in the shop
knew not to disturb J.C. when his soaps were
on. If he were to be disturbed, it had better
be important. Especially since the results of
the paternity test for Tina's newborn baby
girl would be made known today, revealing
either Trent or Felton as the father. Under
order of the Court, all three had been
directed to take a DNA test to determine
paternity.

Tina was J.C.'s type of tramp, and he
had waited nine months for this revelation.
Today's episode had all of his attention.

Kazi, J.C.'s most trusted bodyguard,
knocked on the door, disengaging J.C. from
his trance. "J.C.," said Kazi from the door,
body half in and half out.

J.C. ignored him, eyes fixated on the
television screen.

The woman on TV said, "Trent, you know
I'll always love you, no matter what the
result of that test is. This will always be

your—our child."

"*J.C.*," Kazi said a little louder with an ounce of stress in his voice.

With his eyes still fixed on the television, in a low, slow tone, J.C. answered, "What?"

"Um, a policeman is here to see you."

"Does he have a search warrant?"

"No, but…"

"Then tell him to go the fuck away. Now I'm busy. Fuck off."

"Tina," the man on television replied, "the baby has to be mine. I can feel that it is. It just has to be or…I don't know how I will go on."

"J.C.," he replied with a sound of urgency in his voice, "it's Noble."

Noble was a detective for the Metro-Dade Police Department. His street name was "Noble" because everyone on the street knew that he took "No Bull" and that he played "No Bull." He always played it straight by the street rules. Therefore, his name became, Noble.

J.C. swung his head around. "Noble? Shit." It was the first time that J.C. had taken his eyes off of the television screen. "Damn." J.C. knew full well that Noble never needed a warrant. Noble had enough on J.C. from the past ten years to lock him up for the rest of his life as well as his grandchildren's lives. J.C. retorted, "Send him in." He hit the record button on his DVR and clicked the television off.

Noble made his way through the narrow hall to the back room where J.C. sat at a card table. The room had no windows and wood paneling covered all four walls causing the room to be dark and quiet. There were three card tables with chairs, one large 50-inch flat screen television, and lots of calculators lying around. This was the room where Rawlings's Liberty City drug money was counted on late Tuesday nights into Wednesday morning when it was to be picked up.

Noble pimp-walked past Kazi, smirking at him as if to say, "Damn straight. I'm Noble and you better always remember that." White, six foot three and just entering his mid-forties, one could tell that back in the day he used to be pure muscle. However, time had begun to show its effect and good conscious should have told him, at least two years ago, that his shirt was too tight.

He walked over to J.C.'s table and sat down next to him.

J.C. both respected Noble and feared him. Noble never took any shit. However, Noble always kept his word. If Noble said he was going to look the other way, he would look the other way. J.C. would use his knowledge of the people on the street to help Noble solve his crimes, and Noble would allow J.C. to operate without serious police intervention. So long as J.C. kept the information coming on other criminals, Noble left him alone.

When Noble needed to talk to J.C., however, he would usually do it on the sly. Slip through the back window or door so J.C. would not be labeled a snitch.

But today was different. Noble boldly entered through the front door. As a result J.C. figured that something heavy was going down and Noble didn't have any time to waste.

"Noble, baby," J.C. said in an apprehensive tone. "What can I do for you today?"

Noble moved close to J.C., slapping him on the back. "Last Wednesday somebody stole a *whole* lot of money from here." He looked J.C. in the eyes and paused.

J.C. began to fidget. Was Noble working for Rawlings or the police department? Was Rawlings now insinuating through Noble that J.C. had something to do with the theft? J.C. could feel his body temperature rising.

Noble kept his stare hard and cold. He paused a bit longer and then continued. "And three people were killed in the process." Noble smacked J.C. on the back again and began pacing the room. "I don't want to get into where the money came from. If I wanted to know that, I could find out. And I know you don't want to tell me that. So, to make things easier, I won't go there. You can keep me from those questions, if you just tell me what I want to know."

"Anything you need, baby, you know this."

Noble stopped pacing as his voice dropped even lower. "Who stole the money?"

J.C., distraught, looked up at Noble. "You know I'm always on the up and up with you, and if——"

Irritation flashed across Noble's face. He picked up the table that J.C. sat at and thrust it at the wall, causing it to crackle and splinter into useless debris. Frigid and helpless, J.C. sat there, scared stiff.

Noble lifted J.C.'s precious television

above his head and thrust it to the ground, cracking the screen. When it hit the ground J.C. winched and pursed his lips. "I'm looking for something else to break!"

J.C. froze. His face looked ashen and his toes curled back in his shoes. Never had he seen Noble act in such a way towards him; he wasn't quite sure how to respond.

Noble stood over the television looking at its broken pieces on the floor, panting. Trying to compose himself he lifted his head.

In a hushed voice, he said, "All I want to know is who stole the fucking money."

J.C. had no answer.

Noble began to lose it again. "Stop all the bullshit! Either tell me, or get your toothbrush right now, because you are going to jail!"

J.C. stood, raising his hands to his side. "Noble, man, please, calm down. I don't know who stole it. I swear."

Noble picked up another chair and hurled it against the wall, causing the paneling to crack. "Don't fuck with me, man! Turn around; you're coming downtown!" He spun J.C. around and with Olympic speed, handcuffed him.

"Wait, Noble, my man! I may be able to help you, if you just give me a second."

Noble ignored his desperate plea. "You have the right to remain in jail for the next fucking decade or so and anything you say can and will be used against you—"

"Noble!"

Noble had him by the wrists from behind and began strong arming J.C. to the door. As they shuffled towards the door, J.C. knew he was going to be in jail for a long time unless he did something quick.

J.C. shouted in fear for his life, "Noble, man! Come on! I said I got something!"

Noble stopped for a short second. He put his mouth next to J.C.'s ear. "You better have something good. You know I don't bullshit around."

"Listen." The fear in J.C.'s throat made his voice crack. "You've got to take the cuffs off to let me show you."

Noble looked at him as if he was crazy.

"Where the fuck I'm gonna run to? You find me all the time when I don't want to be found. Come on, think. I *always* level with you, 'cause I know you don't play no bullshit."

Noble unlocked the handcuffs. "Okay. Show me what you got to show me. And it better be good."

"Two things," J.C. said as he rubbed his wrists where the cuffs had held him. He went over to the safe and attempted to unlock it. His hands shook, so it took him longer to open it than usual. Finally, the lock popped opened and he pulled out a shell casing.

"This is a shell casing from the gun he had." He held it out to Noble like it was being entered into evidence at trial.

Noble smacked the casing out of his hand. "What the fuck is that?"

J.C. didn't answer.

With his teeth pulled back in a snarl, he answered his own question. "I'll tell you what that is. That's a useless piece of shit. Just like you."

"I ain't done. Man, what's wrong with

you? You don't have no patience today——"

"I don't have time to be patient, so you had better show me something good, and soon."

J.C. took Noble outside to the front of the barbershop. He stood right where the van stopped for the pickup. J.C. pointed across the street.

"See there. The bank. I couldn't get the info, but you being a policeman and all, it should be no problem."

"What the fuck are you talking about?"

"Right there." He pointed. "The ATM machine. There's a camera in there, and it's looking right out onto this area."

Noble locked in like he had a gun sight in his eyes on the ATM across the street. His body relaxed a bit, as the tell-tale lines of stress left his forehead.

He looked at J.C. with a devilish smile. "Very, very, good. I knew I could count on you."

* * *

Two hours later Noble walked into the Liberty City branch of the Bank of Miami armed with an information subpoena. He made his way through the lobby over to the loan officer area. Although there were at least a half dozen people waiting to be seen, Noble cut in front of them all to a loan officer taking an application.

"Yes, may I help you?" the loan officer stated, visibly offended by his complete disregard for the people waiting.

Noble, cool as ever, pulled out his badge and stuck it in her face. "Police officer, ma'am. Is the manager in?"

The loan officer, taken back by the
badge, changed her attitude from one of
snobbish resentment to one of helpfulness.
She looked at the people sitting on the other
side of her desk and said, "Would you please
excuse me for a moment?"

With that she smiled at Noble and asked
him to follow her. "The bank manager's name
is Mark Jacobsen. He's right back this way."

She walked Noble through the cubicle
area and into the office area where the offices
had doors and windows of their own.

When they finally arrived at the
manager's office, he sat on the phone with his
feet kicked up on the desk massaging the back
of his neck with his right hand.

He rattled pleasant conversation into
the phone as Noble and the loan officer
arrived at the door. He looked up and saw the
two standing at his door.

"Ted," he said, "let me get back to you
on that… Yeah, okay… Bye." As he ended his
conversation he directed his attention to the
loan officer. "Martha, what can I do for you,"
he said with a cheesy businessman smile.

"This man here," she pointed with the
palm of her hand, "is a police officer and
would like to speak with you for a moment."

"Police officer? Well, come on in and
sit down." He came from around his desk to
give a warmer welcome to his guest. He shook
Noble's hand and introduced himself. "Is
there anything I can get for you? Coffee,
tea, soda?"

With an impetuous edge Noble replied,
"No thank you, but there is something else

that I need."

# CHAPTER SEVEN
Monday 5:05 p.m. Day 8.
August 9, 2010


The clock read 5:05 p.m. and almost everyone, except Ben, had left the courthouse for the day. As a general rule, the courthouse employees would clear out at 5:00 sharp, everyday.

However, for Ben, his work day would continue until well into the evening. The mountain of motions still sat before him on his desk. He had worked all day long and had only completed five of the forty-nine motions.

He wanted to know if Dana had tried to text him, so for the tenth time today he checked to see if his cell phone service had been restored. To his dismay, he found that it had not. Because he had made an online payment on Saturday he felt that by now his service should've been restored.

Agitated, he shoved the phone back into his pocket, took a sip of hot tea and got back down to business.

The motion on which he was currently working was a typical, boring, domestic relations motion.

Despite the tea, Ben's mind went back

to the $25,000 proposition. He tried to throw the thought out of his mind, but it persisted. Twenty-five thousand dollars. He could catch up on his student loans, he thought. Pay off his credit cards so he wouldn't have to use a poker face while waiting to see if the charge went through. Pay off his car. Even go on a vacation, something he hadn't done in over twenty years.

Ben caught himself wandering and tried to focus back on his work. He closed his eyes and re-gathered his thoughts and tried to concentrate. It was mandatory that he get this work done. If not, the judge would rip his ass apart. Taking a deep breath, he put all of his energy into making the mountainous pile leaner.

"The money would be so easy," a whispered inner-voice told him.

He sat there in thought, blinking his eyes, staring at the top of his desk.

The voice continued. "You know where the key to the evidence room is. Yeah. It's in the judge's desk in the top middle draw. It'll be so easy."

He sat there as his subconscious mapped out how he could get the key out of the judge's desk, walk over to the evidence room, look through some boxes and search for one of the alleged memos.

The image was so vivid that he felt as though he had already gone in and found the memo. His eyes darted in the direction of the evidence room. Then, better judgment began to rise up in his mind, snapping him back to reality.

No way would he do that. Out of the
question. The money was not worth the risk,
he told himself.

There.

With that in mind, he put his head back
down into his work and continued to read on.
Ben let out a long, stretching yawn.

"The evidence room is right there," the
voice told him.

Ben looked across the foyer to the door
which read: Evidence Room. Now, even from
across the room, the thin stenciled letters
seemed larger than usual, as though they were
looming from the door panel, written in bold.

"Yes, see it?" the voice asked.

On its own volition, his head nodded a
response. The room sat ever so silent and the
building calm. The evidence door just stood
there, tempting Ben like chocolate to a fat
kid.

He began to recall how those memos had
made their way into the evidence room in the
first place. A few weeks earlier he remembered
Alyse telling him about the phone conference
that Judge Pomerence had with the Killinger's
attorneys.

Mrs. Killinger had been vacationing at
the family beach house at Deer Key. Her
attorney told Judge Pomerance that she was
looking through storage boxes, looking for
family photos. The pending divorce litigation
had her reminiscing.

As she foraged through the photo boxes,
she ran across the memos.

As she read the memos, she understood
that the Overton Industries' value was
substantially more than what her husband

had revealed through the discovery process.
In fact, very few people knew that Overton
Industries was on the cusp of a technological
breakthrough that could change the entire
agricultural and socio-economic landscape in
every third world country with access to salt
water.

Mrs. Killinger did not care so much about
the third world countries and the benefit this
technology held for them. She understood one
thing: If this new technology, wholly owned
by Overton Industries was not known to the
investment institutions, then the value of
Overton Industries stock was undervalued, by
millions, if not billions of dollars.

Her logic followed, that if Overton
Industry stock remained lower than what
it should be, and she received a divorce
settlement based upon the value of that
stock, she would, herself, be losing millions
of dollars. Who knows, she thought, maybe
billions.

Under no circumstances would she to let
that happen. She had not spent the last 38
years of her life with that bastard to let
him rip her off like that.

So, she packed up all of the memos, and
every other Overton Industries box she could
find, and took them directly to her attorney's
office.

Her attorney called Mr. Killinger's
attorney who threatened him with words like
"SEC prosecution" and "insider trading."
Mrs. Killinger's attorney had been personal
friends with Martha Stewart and did not want
to end up in jail like her. So, they agreed
to ask Judge Pomerance to keep the files in

his chambers, under seal, until such time the issue of the memos and their relationship to the divorce and SEC regulations could be determined. The Judge agreed that would be the prudent course of action.

Judge Pomerance and Ben dealt with a docket of at least 500 active divorce cases at any one time. When the files first arrived into the judge's chambers it did not seem like a big deal to Ben. Business as usual.

Now, it was all he could think of.

Just then his desk phone rang. Ben snatched it up, hoping that it would, somehow be Dana.

"Benjamin?"

"Yes?"

"This is Slobodoan."

*Damn,* Ben thought. Slobodan Jakov, his landlord. Ben knew exactly why he was calling. Rent was due eight days ago, and Ben hadn't paid. Ben really enjoyed his job as a law clerk and had learned a ton about the reality of law in the past eleven months. But the meager pay for a law clerk in Florida should have been outlawed by the Thirteenth Amendment which abolished slavery. The pay was slim and simply not enough to cover all of Ben's monthly expenses.

Ben hemmed and hawed his way through the phone call promising to pay within the next few days.

Slobodan had always been polite to Ben, so it wasn't hard for Ben convince him he would pay him and get off the phone quickly. Ben hated the fact that robbing Peter to pay Paul had become his lifestyle.

He shook his head and pounded his fist on

the desk. He found himself headed across the room to the judge's desk grabbing the key and heading into the evidence closet.

He unlocked the door and turned the light on. He stood there for a moment, mentally checking in with himself to see if he was really doing this. *Yes, I think I am,* he thought.

He walked through the rows of boxes and tidbits of evidence until he came upon the shelves with the name "Killinger" stuck to them with adhesive tape.

There were 92 boxes in all. Ben knew this could take some time, so he started at one end and began to methodically work his way through each and every box. Each box was filled with all kinds of information and financial reports that Ben simply did not understand.

There were profit projection analysis charts, spreadsheets, market research reports, even some prospectuses on other companies.

An hour and a half later, when Ben hit the thirty-seventh box, he ran across it; a piece of paper in a bright red folder. Across the top of the folder it read:

MEMORANDUM C (Highly sensitive - do not disseminate)

It was one of the memos Darren Hall had inquired about. Ben sighed with relief. He looked in the folder and the paper inside had the same heading as the folder.

After reading the heading and enough of the memorandum's contents to know it was what Mr. Hall wanted he quickly found his way over

to the printer and burned off a copy. As fast
as he could he made his way back into the
evidence room and placed everything back the
way he'd found it. He folded his copy of the
memo into a square and neatly placed it into
his back pocket. He left the evidence closet,
put the key back in the judge's desk, and
walked back to his desk, feeling a bit more
satisfied.

Now he could at least concentrate on
his work. He knew that he did not have to
give Darren Hall anything if he did not want
to. But at least he had the option now. He
had until ten o'clock tonight to decide
what to do, if anything, with this newfound
information.

# CHAPTER EIGHT

Monday evening. Day 8.
August 9, 2010

Noble expected company, so the knock on the door shouldn't have startled him. But it did. Looking through the peephole he could see Tommy, rocking back and forth, waiting. He let Tommy slide through.

"Did anybody follow you?" Noble asked.

"No."

"Are you sure?"

"Yes, I'm sure," Tommy answered, almost offended at the question.

Noble opened the door again and stuck his head out. He looked both ways outside the door for a perfunctory inspection. He didn't see anything unusual, so he shut the door.

Tommy immediately inquired, "Do you know who stole the money yet?"

"Yes and no."

Tommy looked confused. "What the f——" He stopped himself. "What do you mean, 'yes and no'?"

"First, I want to make sure that the reward is still one hundred thousand."

Tommy seemed a bit offended but remained professional. "You are correct. Mr. Rawlings will pay one hundred thousand dollars in cash, to whoever finds the person who stole his money. You need not worry about the money."

"Good."

Noble had jumping beans in his stomach. This would most certainly mean retirement for him. He had considered retiring and moving to some type of tropical island, maybe with coconut and mango trees growing outside his door. There, he would wear nothing but swimming trunks and sip cheap cocktails all day long. For fun, he figured he would work, part-time, maybe as a scuba-diving tour guide and instructor. He hadn't been able to decide just exactly how he would spend the rest of his time.

But whatever he did, it would be the life. The closest he would ever come to solving another crime would be to watch the TV show *CSI: Miami*.

"I have a video of the suspect, but it's blurry. I can't figure out his identity."

"Well then, let's see the video."

Both men sat down at the table in front of the DVD player.

Noble inquired, "Want a beer? I got some in the fridge."

"No thanks," Tommy replied. He was there on business.

Noble grabbed one for himself and sat down at the table with Tommy. He reached for the remote and pressed play as he sucked down half of his beer. A black and white image appeared on the screen. The resolution and quality of the image was awful.

They could see the front door of Mr. G's

Barbershop. Tommy inched a little closer to
the screen when he saw the image appear.

A couple of cars passed by. Some
pedestrians walked through the camera's field
of view. Then a van, with no side windows,
pulled up in front of Mr. G's Barbershop. The
van sat there parked for a minute or two.
Then, a dark figure wearing a baggy shirt and
a baseball cap appeared at the van with a gun
in hand. It showed Demetrius pushing Joshua,
shooting him in the head and climbing over
his body into the van.

Shortly thereafter, in a jolt, the van
disappeared from the camera's view. The video
ended.

Tommy looked over at Noble. "You can't
tell who that fucking guy is from that. The
picture quality is hideous. I mean, is that
it?"

Noble, in a reassuring voice said, "No,
that's not it."

"Well, I tell you, it sure didn't look
like a hell of a lot."

"Wait one moment," Noble said as he
pressed the back button. All the prior action
occurred in reverse on the screen. Noble
paused the DVD player on one of the frames
where the culprit was approaching Joshua from
behind. For two or three frames, the camera
caught a side profile of the culprit.

Tommy belted out, "Why in the world
would any asshole make a security camera for
an ATM that takes video so bad you can't tell
who the vandal is from the damn video? Who we
ought to kill is the asshole at the bank who
bought that camera."

Tommy made an on-point assessment

regarding the camera's picture quality. The lack of detail in the video appeared to make the image of the assailant seem useless.

"Wait. This is not the end, by any stretch of the imagination," Noble reassured Tommy. "We know he is African American, and gauging his height in relation to the height of the van, we can tell he's about six feet two inches tall."

"Wow! That narrows it down to what? Half of Miami's population? Good work!" Tommy rolled his eyes.

Noble ignored the remark. "And most importantly, I can send this image to the lab for digital enhancement."

That caught Tommy's attention.

"And then, once the enhancement comes back, I can use the police computer to analyze this picture and match it with any existing mug shots in our file. I mean, I'm sure that this guy has had a prior run in with the law. He doesn't come across as a first-time criminal. This guy had to be well-seasoned. Well-seasoned and have a big-ass pair of balls. And if he has been into some shit before, we have his mug shot on file. And if we have his mug shot, the computer *will* make a match on it." Noble smiled at Tommy.

"How long will it take before the lab enhances this DVD?"

"About three or four days. I'll pull some strings to get it done as soon as possible."

Tommy rubbed his chin. He jumped to his feet and held out his hand to Noble. "Thanks, detective. I appreciate you working on this in a confidential manner. I'll advise Mr.

Rawlings of your progress and, of course, once we have that man's name, we will forward the money to you."

Tommy shook his hand and headed for the door. Watching Tommy leave the hotel room, Noble sucked down the remainder of his beer with a content smile on his face.

August 9, 2010
Monday 10:00 p.m.
Day 8

It was as though he were a character in a script and someone he didn't know or understand was doing the writing and making all the decisions. Furtively rubbing his hands together he noticed that a sweaty balm had begun to coat his palms. Lost deep in thought he acknowledged that he was outside of himself, watching and studying himself, wondering what he would do next.

Like an alien spaceship burning through the atmosphere and crash landing on earth, unusual events and circumstances had come crashing into his otherwise routine and monotonous life. One day his life was a bunch of motions, briefs and bill collectors; a week later it was full of sex and offers of money. Never in a million years would he have expected to have such chaotic stir visited upon him. Even less expected was that he would have responded the way he had and this perplexed him.

"Why am I here?" he asked himself. "Is this really me, here on this beach, getting ready to do this?" *Two weeks ago,* he thought, *I would've known exactly why I was here and what I would do next. Right now, anyone's guess is as good as mine.*

These thoughts and feelings were totally new to him, and it made him nervous such that he simply could not sit still. Though he wasn't a nail biter, he wished at this point he had been just so his body had something to do.

So Ben pensively waited in the humid night air, waiting for Darren Hall to appear. After pacing and fidgeting for the past five minutes he had found a seat under the light on the retaining wall and looked out onto the people on the strip. His mind again pondered the issue of his personal safety.

Monday night had never been a big crowd draw on South Beach, but still, there were enough people walking the strip to make him feel that if he had to yell for help, he would be heard.

From the darkness of the beach Darren approached Ben's backside tapping him on the shoulder. Turning around startled Ben snapped, "What the hell?"

Briefcase in hand Darren replied, "Sorry, I didn't mean to surprise you. My bad."

Intent on getting this thing over and done with Ben cut straight to the chase. Tilting his head toward the briefcase he asked, "What do you got for me there?"

Darren replied, "Do you have my information?"

"Maybe. Actually, I haven't made up my mind yet. I want to see the money first, make sure it's all there."

"Have it your way."

Darren clicked open the briefcase, sat it on the retaining wall, and flipped through the bundles of cash. Ben took a bill from the middle of a few bundles verifying that the red and green fibers were removable. Ben then held the bills up to the light, insuring that they had the proper watermarks. Satisfied that the money wasn't counterfeit, he returned the bills to the briefcase.

He wondered if it actually amounted to twenty-five thousand dollars. He doubted if Darren would stand there and wait for him to count each individual bill. It looked like a lot of money, and under the circumstances, Ben figured that he'd have to trust Darren's word.

For the umpteenth time, Ben allowed his paranoid eyes to scan both the stretching shore of the beach and the strip. As best as he could tell, 'Big Brother' wasn't watching. But what if this was a setup, a sting operation to get rid of the crooks in the justice system? Ben's eyes swept the man's appearance for any tell-tale signs that he was a narc. He didn't look like an officer, but that didn't mean he wasn't.

Ben asked, "Are you a cop?"

As he adjusted his glasses, Darren laughed. "Hell no."

That put some of Ben's worry at ease. Ben knew that if Darren Hall was a cop, he was required by law to admit it. If he was lying about his occupation, Ben could use the entrapment defense to beat any charges filed against him.

But still, something didn't quite feel right. Ben's inner-voice said, "This money is too easy." Like an oscillating radar antenna, Ben looked around the beach again.

"Okay," Ben said after a few more seconds of indecision. "I'm gonna need a minute or two to think through this thing again and make sure that I'm doing the right thing here."

Darren Hall held his hands out to the side. "Fair enough."

\* \* \*

Ben played a central, integral role in the grand plan of Darren Hall. Darren had been following the personal life of Walt

Killinger for years, hoping to discover, from any of his actions, something that might make money for Darren on the stock market.

He knew Killinger's wife had discovered something important, and that "something important" had been delivered to Judge Pomerance's chambers. He knew that as a matter of law, all documents filed in a divorce action were to be available for public review. But the Killinger papers had been sealed by the court and placed in the evidence room.

To Darren, the fact that they were sealed meant that the value of the documents were in their secrecy. From what he had gleaned from his research as well as blogs and online chats, those documents most likely dealt with the future plans of Overton Industries. That meant access to the evidence room could make Demetrius a rich man.

Ben had access to that room, and Darren needed access to Ben, so he would be as patient on that beach with Ben as he needed to be.

* * *

Once again, Ben took a long, nervous scan of his surroundings. There were still a lot of people out mulling around the shops and restaurants but nothing unusual stood out. Ninety-nine point nine percent sure he had made his decision, with a quick flick Ben closed the briefcase and faced Darren.

"Okay," he said like it was a confession. "I found one of those memos in the evidence room."

"All right!" Darren Hall quietly said to himself, clapping his hands together hard one time. With bated breath he asked Ben, "Can I see it?"

Ben reached into his pocket and unfolded the memo. Before handing it over to Darren, again, he took one last look around him to see if anyone was looking, but again, to him, everything seemed normal. Taking a deep breath he realized handing that memo over to Darren meant crossing the point of no return. He silently asked himself, "Are you sure this is what you want to do?"

He stretched his hand out to Darren.

After taking possession of the memo Darren scoured the entire document with the fervor of a lion eating its prey. With a look of unadulterated satisfaction he looked up and said, "Thank you, Ben. This is a good thing you have done."

"Yeah, right. Good luck with your lawsuit," Ben quickly replied. Becoming more paranoid by the second he was more than ready to clear the area, so with no delay he turned and disappeared into the crowd on the strip, briefcase clutched tightly in his hand. Likewise, Darren Hall slipped back into the darkness of the beach.

Cutting a brisk pace through the steamy Miami night air Ben's focus was straight ahead and stern. As he bobbed in and out of people on the sidewalk Ben's mind began to assess what had just occurred. His face began to grow pensive and his eyes sunken. A voice from somewhere deep inside his psyche spoke up and advised Ben that he had just broken the law. Which law exactly he was not sure, but he was positive it involved a prison term of some sort.

The greed side of his psyche didn't give a damn, but the logic side started to immediately regret what Ben had done.

He began chastising himself as he thought, *I should've never given Darren Hall that memo. That was the single dumbest thing I have ever done in my entire life.*

A bit too late for it to do him any good Ben fully realized that he had been blinded by greed. Now that greed had accomplished its goal it began to recede to the point where it no longer clouded Ben's logic. As a result, logic had gained 20/20 vision and it began to work him over with introspective thoughts of possible consequences.

What if Darren Hall was not who he said he was? What if the information he gave him showed up on the front page of the *New York Times* or *Huffingtonpost.com*? A huge investigation could be instituted and eventually, Ben could be implicated.

What if it was a police sting operation aimed at cleaning up corruption in the judicial system? The entrapment defense, his logic asked, do you really believe that would work? Get real.

What if Darren Hall actually was a reporter for *Dateline NBC* or *Wikileaks.com*? Ben realized he had exposed himself in more ways than he had ever considered beforehand.

At that moment, as if it were an epiphany, logic revealed to him who was writing the script. It was his psyche, with greed on one side and logic on the other,

both making suggestions to the psyche, line
by line. The goal of the psyche being to
write a script were in the end, Ben would be
safe, secure, and loved.

Despite everything that his logic was
now telling him, greed remained satisfied
and without regret, having obtained what it
wanted. Greed had coerced Ben into taking
the money because that is what greed wanted,
whatever consequences may come. Greed held
the position that consequences aren't my
responsibility. If logic let me convince Ben
to take the money, then it is logic's duty to
deal with the consequences.

That's exactly what Ben would have to do
because right now, that was the most logical
thing to do. And unless he was caught in a
sting, logic meant paying his bills with that
money.

* * *

By the time he reached his apartment
building, he had sweat stains stamped into
the armpits of his shirt. Stepping off the
third flight of stairs to his apartment, he
saw a pair of slender, sultry legs sticking
out into the hallway. He turned the corner to
see her sitting there, bringing a feeling of
immense pleasure to him.

Ah, Dana.

His face lit up like a Christmas tree
and he was taken aback with joy like one
who walks in on their own surprise birthday
party.

She sat there stoic, with her back
against the door to his apartment. She looked

exhausted to Ben.

He asked, "Hey, you okay?"

She looked up. "Hi, baby." The smile looked contrived.

"I've been missing you like crazy," Ben confessed.

"Then why didn't you respond to any of my texts?"

He felt too ashamed to tell her that his phone had been cut off. "My phone charger broke."

"Humph," she responded under her breath. "Can I come in?"

He unlocked the door as Dana filed in behind him. She made her way to his kitchen, opened his refrigerator and began to scan the contents. Ben headed directly to his bedroom.

She called out to him, "Do you want some wine?"

"Why not," he shouted back as he looked for a quick place to set the money.

Refusing to keep her waiting long he set the brief case under the bed as a temporary hiding spot. It was the best place he could think of at the moment. He changed into a clean, dry shirt then walked back into the living room as Dana entered from the kitchen.

She had a glass full of wine in each hand. She sat down and handed Ben a glass. Silence stretched between them and though he knew she felt his eyes on her, she wouldn't look at him.

Finally, to break the silence, Ben said, "So, how have you been?"

It was a while before she answered. "Ben, why don't you have a girlfriend?"

"Who says I don't have a girlfriend? I

never said that I didn't have a girlfriend."

She shot a glance at him with one brow lifted high.

"I don't have a girlfriend," he responded.

A slight smile appeared on her face. "I must've texted you a thousand times this weekend. I figured you weren't responding because you were with someone else."

Is that why she's acting so aloof, he asked himself.

"I just really needed to talk to you this weekend, baby, and I couldn't. I missed you."

"I guess I could've called from a landline, but I didn't want to call at the wrong time. You know, with you being married and all."

"Baby, it's okay." She took a sip of wine.

"What were you so anxious to talk to me about this weekend?"

Sounding frustrated she responded, "The moment has passed. It's too late now."

Ben could see that emotionally, she was vulnerable. He really wanted to know her personal details, and he felt that now would be a good time to strike while the coals were hot.

"Obviously you're not happy at home, or else you wouldn't be over here with me."

She remained silent.

"Do you really want to leave him, or are you just saying that to keep me around?"

She pursed her lips tighter.

Ben continued to dig, "I don't know how you feel about me, and, I must confess, I like you…a lot. But, this secrecy thing…"

"Ben——" She knelt on her knees in front of him, grabbed his hand and looked him in the eye for the first time. "There's so much going on in my life right now. You don't understand."

"I'd like to."

"Not too many questions tonight, okay?" She did not wait for an answer as she laid her head in his lap. "Just hold me."

His disappointment was obvious, but against his better judgment, he decided to let the issue ride this one last time.

Eventually, Ben and Dana went to the bedroom, but when he started kissing her and undoing her blouse, she stopped him. She didn't want to have sex. She simply wanted to be held. Feeling obliged not to disappoint her Ben pulled her close and soon enough she fell asleep in his arms.

Ben, however, had difficulty sleeping. He watched Dana for a while until he could confirm that she was locked in a deep sleep. He then got up so he could tend to the twenty-five grand sitting under his bed. At the moment, the best spot he could think of was the cupboard in the kitchen, well hidden behind the non-perishables. He secured the money there.

Temporarily satisfied with the location of the money, his curiosity of Dana got the best of him. He made his way back into the bedroom and over to where Dana's jeans and purse lay on a chair. He began checking them both for some sort of ID, but she didn't have her wallet on her. He only found a fifty dollar-bill rolled up in her jeans pocket.

He picked up her cell phone and clicked it on, but it was pass code protected. Somewhat agitated, he put the phone back down.

He then went to the living room and turned on his Mac Book Pro. He googled Dana Selvey and over 75 names popped up. None of them were his Dana. The same thing happened when he tried her name on Facebook and Myspace. He then searched her name on the white pages, but found no positive results. Lastly, he entered her cell phone number into a cell phone database, which displayed that a match had been made, but in order to see the match, he had to pay $1.99.

Feeling ecstatic, Ben paid the amount via PayPal, and as soon as he pressed the "go" button, the screen displayed the following message:

**The attempt was unsuccessful.
You will not be charged for this inquiry.**

His shoulders slumped down as he read the reply. Looking at the bright side of the situation he appreciated that at least he hadn't wasted two dollars.

After a half hour of more unsuccessful research, he crept back into bed with Dana and lay next to her. The clock read 5:37 a.m. when Dana awoke from sleep. When she opened her eyes, Ben was laying on his pillow gazing at her.

"Hey," he said smiling.

"Hey, you. What are you doing?" she said in a soft voice as she caressed the side of his face.

"Watching sleeping beauty."

Dana laughed.

"You look so serene when you sleep," Ben said.

"Yeah, when I'm with you."

Ben's tone turned more serious. "Babe, you seemed pretty upset last night."

"I was upset."

"Is that why you came by?"

"No. I came by because I couldn't stop thinking about you, and you didn't text me back all weekend."

"Well, that's a good thing."

"Why is that good?"

"Because I can't get you off my mind, either."

The edge of her lips turned upward, barely revealing the start of a smile. "You know, Ben, it feels good to have a connection with somebody. It's so rare."

She rolled herself closer to Ben, and whispered, "Is it my imagination, or did we connect Friday night?"

Ben was about to answer when he was interrupted by the buzz of Dana's phone. Ogling at the screen, her face took on a blank stare. She read the number then closed her eyes tight and grimaced as she dropped her head down onto the pillow. She took a deep breath and readied herself as she clicked the phone on.

"Hello, Mommy." She tried to force her voice to sound relaxed. "Mommy, slow down, I can't hear what you're saying." She paused. "Mom, stop crying. I can't understand what you——" She sighed. "What did you say to Daddy to make him do that to you?" More silence.

"I'm sure you said something. What did you do?" She sounded frustrated. "Why didn't you do what he said?" She massaged her temple. "I believe you, but what did you expect?" She stopped speaking long enough for her mom to respond. "Where's dad?" She closed her eyes. "Did you apologize?" She exhaled and ran her hand through her hair. "Why not?" She didn't wait for a response before adding, "Mommy, you have to apologize. Just apologize. It'll be okay." She remained quiet as she listened. "Does it hurt?" She opened her eyes and glanced at Ben. "You didn't have to go to the hospital did you?" She looked away. "Good. *Whenever* dad gets home ask him to give me a call." She rolled her eyes. "Mom, I gotta go. I love you too." She clicked the phone off.

Though the volume on her phone wasn't loud enough that he could hear her mother's responses, he had listened intently to Dana's words. He asked, "What the hell was that?"

Running her fingers through her hair she said, "That was my mom."

"I know that." Ben frowned at her. "Is she okay? What's going on between your mom and dad?"

She ignored his questions.

He dug again. "Why did you tell her to apologize?"

As if to issue a warning she stated, "Ben, leave it alone."

He pressed more. "If your dad hit your mom, why did you tell *her* to apologize?" Ben waited for an answer.

Quietly, she responded, "That's how things are there. You wouldn't understand."

"I'm all ears, babe. Explain it to me."

"I gotta pee."

She exited the bed and disappeared into the bathroom. She took the bed sheet with her leaving Ben naked and exposed. While she was gone, Ben started to add things up. Upon her return, she laid in the bed with her back to Ben.

Ben clamored over close to her as he asked, "Dana, does your husband hit you?"

She lay there, ice still, refusing to answer.

"Does he?" he asked again.

Not quite under her breath she muttered, "Not when I do as he asks."

Her answer began to sink into Ben when Dana's cell phone buzzed again. According to the screen, it was a text message. He wondered if it was her husband.

She rolled on her side so that Ben couldn't see what the text stated. As she read it, her body tensed up. Jumping out of the bed she began to gather her belongings.

"What's up?" Ben inquired.

"I have to go."

"Why, what's going on?"

"That was my husband. He's back early, and I've gotta go pick him up from the airport." She started dressing herself.

"You've got to get away from him," Ben exclaimed.

"Leave him so we can fall in love? Come on. Get real." She continued getting dressed.

Her words offended him but right now Ben's concern wasn't about his feelings; it was about her willingly placing her life and health in danger. "This isn't about us, Dana. This is about you living *your* life."

"Your sister thought the same thing, and look what it got her." Her statement stung Ben to the core. Still, she wasn't ready to relent as she continued, "You have no right to tell me how to live my life, Ben. And best I can tell, you have no life."

This time, her words cut to the white meat. Defensively, he said, "That's not true."

"Oh, no?" She cocked an eyebrow at him. "I see things. You're so afraid of losing someone else, you won't let anyone close. You're a twenty-six year old, good-looking guy. You have a lot going for you, and you don't even have a girlfriend. I don't think you have *any* friends. How many friends do you have, Ben?"

Ben dared not answer. Chalie and Thomas were his only friends, and he had seen them only one time in the past nine months.

She continued to filet and open Ben up as if she were cleaning a fish. "I don't want to be alone, so don't tell me how to live my life." She looked into her compact, checking every aspect of her appearance.

Ben, feeling scathed but undeterred, said, "Refusing to be alone and being abused are two different things."

"If I left my husband, who would take care of me?"

Ben's face looked as confused as it ever had. "Take care of you? You are a grown woman. You're more than capable of taking care of yourself."

The comment seemed to reflect off of Dana's newly exhibited hard shell. "I'm not a loner like you, and I don't intend to end up like your sister."

"I guess your mom has set the mark then."

If looks could kill, Ben would have already taken his last breath.

"Bye, Ben," she uttered as she slammed the door closed behind her.

* * *

As she drove to the airport, Ben's words ate away at her mind like acid slowly burning its way through metal. At 6:51 a.m. the sun began to arise from the east and when she looked into her rearview mirror, she could see the breaking light of dawn. After her spat with Ben she felt different inside. A new day was on the horizon.

Of course, she didn't want to stay under the monocratic rule of her husband. But this way of life represented what she had learned growing up in her particular household. Unlike her mother, however, she had learned how to "behave" and thereby, avoid having to meet the brunt of her husband's punishment.

By learning to behave, she had escaped any serious injury or retribution for at least the past five years. By behaving she had been able to have this relationship with Ben. Had the relationship not been sanctioned by her husband, she had absolutely no doubt at all that she would have never met Ben.

At that very moment the relationship that had planted a small seed inside her heart had begun to grow. Having someone else on the outside see what she had been hiding caused a small fissure in the box which had held the secret for so long, and a small beam of light had broken through.

She drove into the waiting parking lot at the airport and called her husband.

In a voice that seemed to exhibit that all was well in her world, she said, "Honey, I'm in the waiting lot. Let me know when you're out front."

By mid-afternoon the sun shone bright. There wasn't a cloud in the sky and Dana couldn't hold any other thought in her head except the conversation that she'd had with Ben earlier that morning. For some reason, it had left her feeling unsettled. When she could no longer resist she took out her cell and called him.

"Babe, I'm sorry."

Ben talked in a soft, low tone. "I guess things got a bit intense this morning?" She detected an inflection in his voice that told her he was happy to hear from her.

"Yes. I said some things that I regret."

"I think we both may have overstepped our boundaries."

"What you learned about me and my family this morning, I know it sounds crazy, but I don't want to deal with it. Like, if I don't talk about it, it kind of doesn't exist. Do you know what I mean?"

"I do. We both have issues."

*It seems too comfortable,* she thought. *He used the word we. He took some of the blame. He's not real. This isn't real. And he makes me feel…alive.*

She had called to tell Ben that maybe they should cool things down for a bit, but after hearing his voice, she changed her mind. She

would go with the flow and she got right to
it.

"When can I see you again?"

She could hear the smile in his voice.
"Besides work, I'm at your service."

"My husband has announced he wants to
go away down to Key West with me for a couple
of days. Can I call you when I get back?"

"I'll be here, waiting."

"And I'll be thinking about you."

The line was silent until Ben chimed
back, "Dana?"

"Yeah?"

"Be safe."

"I will."

His last statement melted her.

# CHAPTER NINE
Wednesday 12:41 p.m. Day 10.
August 11, 2010

All day Tuesday, and up until this point on
Wednesday, thoughts of Dana were dominating
his mind. At just the thought of her name,
he felt warm and fuzzy inside. On Tuesday,
he had begun using the twenty-five thousand
dollars to pay bills. He completely paid off
two credit cards, his past due rent, and
past due student loans. Paying bills and
getting motions done had been constantly
criss-crossing in his mind, but they paled
by comparison in both quality and quantity
of time Ben spent ruminating on Dana. He had
become obsessed.

During Ben's lunch break he found
himself sitting across the desk from Gonzalo,
a private investigator.

"This is who I need to know about,"
Ben said as he plopped the picture down on
the desk. Monday morning Ben thought that
Dana looked so peaceful and quiet he had to
memorialize her with a photo from his iPhone
4. She had looked absolutely stunning as she
slept.

"Okay," the fiftyish, overweight man

said. "What do you want to know about her?"
He dunked a donut into a cup of coffee. His
teeth were tobacco-stained and his mouth
set in a permanent frown from trying to
subconsciously hide his teeth. He chewed with
his mouth open and when he did, he looked
like a pig. He looked up at Ben, waiting for
the answer.

Leaning closer into the desk Ben said,
"Everything. Where she lives, what she does
for a living." He thought about it for a
minute. "Who her husband is and what he does
for living." He paused again. "Everything."

"Everything costs money, son. Are you
going to be able to afford this?" Even though
Ben was only on the other side of the desk,
Gonzalo yelled as if they were in a crowded
room.

"Don't worry about the money. Just get
me the information." He sounded like a junkie
who just had to have his fix and have it soon.

"What's her last name?"

"Selvey."

"What's her first name?"

"Dana."

"Where does she work?"

"I don't know."

"Son, do you know where she hangs out?"

"No. Not really."

There was a long pause. "And you say you
don't know where she lives?" The investigator
seemed to be getting a little concerned.

"No."

"Well, shit. What's her cell phone
number? Do you know that, son?" The
investigator leaned back in his chair,
swiveling from side to side, thinking. He

seemed to be getting frustrated.

Ben paused. "Yes." He scribbled the number down and handed it to the investigator like it was voucher for a pound of pure gold.

Gonzalo glanced at the number. "Son, that there is a pre-paid cell phone number. Damn near untraceable."

A look of question ran across Ben's face. "That's not good, huh?"

"No. Am I to assume that you did your own research on the web and found nothing?"

Ben pensively shook his head.

"Son," he impatiently said through a chunk of coffee-soaked donut, "I need more information than that. The door says I am a private investigator, not a fucking miracle worker." A piece of donut spewed from his mouth, landing on the right side of his desk.

Ben began searching the realms of his mind for any possible bit of information he could use to find Dana.

"I think she's originally from Atlanta. Besides that, all I have is her cell phone number and that picture," Ben stated with his voice resonating with disappointment.

"She's originally from Atlanta? Well, then son, now instead of knowing a half a squat about her, I now know three quarters of a squat about her."

Ben thought, *at least I gave it a try,* before saying, "Thanks for your time."

However, before Ben could stand to leave, Gonzalo grabbed the photo and phone number and said, "This will do."

Ben's face exploded into a beaming grin.

"Now," the investigator said, "I charge one-fifty per hour, and I need a five hundred dollar retainer."

In a resolute tone Ben told him he would return with the money in a half hour. And he did.

# CHAPTER TEN
Thursday. Day 11.
August 12, 2010


Engrossed in his work, the phone rang, startling Ben. This was his personal extension and usually only attorneys knew that number. So, in a million years, Ben hadn't expected to hear the voice of Darren Hall on the line.

He sat there silent. Stunned. Terrified. What in the world could this guy want?

"Benjamin, are you there?"

Ben's eyes scanned the room, searching for any possible onlookers as he hunched his mouth and shoulder a bit closer to the phone.

"Benjamin, I need to——"

"Listen!" Ben interrupted as he yelled in a whisper. "I don't know who the hell you are, but don't you ever call me again, you got that! Especially at work! Do you understand?"

Darren Hall, his voice deep, clear and calm, said, "Meet me at Rick's Bar tonight at 5:30. It would be in your best interest."

"Leave me the hell alone. I'm not meeting you anywhere. You hear me?" Ben said but received no reply. Again he screamed, "I said do you hear me?"

Darren Hall had hung the phone up.

Ben slammed the phone down. He felt that Darren Hall thought he was in control. And that was not good.

"Ben," a familiar voice said from behind him.

He snapped his neck around like a whip and saw Judge Pomerance in his black robe, standing in the door with a look of apprehension on his face. Ben almost fainted. There was no doubt in his mind that the judge had heard every word of his conversation.

With concern in his voice he asked, "Ben, who was that on the phone?"

Ben could only wonder that if the judge had heard all of the conversation, would he be able to figure out that Ben was involved in something he was not supposed to be involved in? He did his best to try to hide the look of guilt that was showing on his face.

He had to think quickly.

"It was some attorney who keeps calling me asking me to give him legal advice when he knows that I'm not allowed to do that. He keeps calling, and I keep telling him not to."

The judge scrunched his thick eyebrows together. There were a number of pet peeves that could cause the judge to instantly hemorrhage. One of the pet peeves, Ben had learned, involved any occurrence when an attorney stepped upon the judge's authority, in any manner or form. One such form would be to give *his* law clerk a hard time.

"Which attorney?" he asked, the groove between his brows deepening even more. "I'll straighten their ass out right now."

Ben felt stuck now. He offered the best explanation he could on such short notice. "He...," Ben stammered, "...he never leaves his name but has this distinctive 'snaizely' voice. Really annoying, but, uh, I don't know his name."

The judge stood there looking puzzled for a moment as his posture slouched. "Well," he said, straightening the collar of his robe, "if he calls again, put me on the line immediately, and I will deal with him." Perturbed and aggravated, the judge headed to the courtroom.

Ben nodded, feeling relief wash over him. He had avoided a bullet. He took a deep breath as he realized that his blood pressure seemed to have spiked.

Analyzing his every word, he assessed the whole situation in his mind to make sure he hadn't said anything that would lead the judge to believe that he had lied to him. He wondered how long Judge Pomerance had been there. It couldn't have been any more than a few seconds at the most. He reassured himself that the judge had heard nothing that would let him know that Ben had done something illegal.

Rather than blaming himself for partaking in the illegal act, he blamed Darren for dangling the temptation in his face and for nearly getting him busted in front of the judge. Anger colored his vision for the rest of the day. He decided that he would indeed meet with Mr. Darren Hall that night at Rick's. And when he did, he would give him a tongue-lashing so thorough that he'd be sorry he ever met Ben in the first place.

"What the hell is this guy thinking, contacting me at work?" Ben said to no one in particular. "Who the hell does he think he is?"

For sure, Ben resolved, he would let this guy have it. At the same time, Ben would be sure not to mention or admit to any of his prior dealings with him just in case Darren had been tapped or wired.

Then another thought entered Ben's mind and he wondered why the thought hadn't occurred to him sooner. He knew nothing about Darren Hall——if that was his real name. Darren Hall knew Ben's name, what he did for a living, his private phone number at work, what was in his judge's evidence closet, and where he caught a drink after work.

All of this he knew about Ben, and the thought scared him. Badly. Bubbling acid gnawed at the inner-lining of his stomach and his lower back began to ache. Time seemed to move so slowly, he could feel his fingernails growing.

Then all sorts of scenarios started playing out in his Ben's head again. What if Darren Hall has been snagged by the authorities and now he's turned State's evidence? This meeting could be bugged.

Or, maybe Darren Hall gets his kicks out of screwing with people and scaring them senseless.

In any case, Ben knew that he had to go meet with him tonight. While there, he would make it explicitly clear that Darren Hall was to never, ever contact him again in his life.

He'd done what Darren had requested, Darren had given him the money, and now the deal was sealed.

After what seemed like the passing of two blue moons, the work day ended and Ben made his way to Rick's.

* * *

Looking for Darren Hall, but trying to appear as though he were looking for no one, Ben worked his way through the a throng of people. The crowded atmosphere increased his anxiety. On this particular evening, Rick's celebrated Cigar Night, and as such, many patrons were smoking cigars. Clouds of cancer circled the air in gray wisps. Anxious as hell, he moved through the thick smokescreen that burned his eyes and nearly caused him to suffocate. Everyone seemed to be engaged in fun and enjoyable conversation, laughing, joking, and drinking shots of something or the other.

Ben continued to make his way through the bar in what seemed to be slow motion, when he spotted a tall, dark, baldheaded black man sitting alone at a table in the far corner of the bar. He wore a black leather jacket making him look sinister, yet respectable.

Through the smoky haze, Ben could not quite see his face, but he didn't need to. He knew exactly who it was.

As if in ecstasy, Darren Hall exhaled a puff from a cigar, took a swig from a shot glass, and grimaced in pleasure as he swallowed. As Ben approached his table, the man looked up.

As though Ben were a casual business acquaintance he said, "Benjamin, have a seat." He smiled at Ben.

"Do I know you?" Ben said, as if confused.

Darren laughed, "Oh, gamesmanship. Enjoyable to the last." His eyes went thin and his voice dropped an octave as he snapped, "Sit down."

Ben looked around for a second or two, checking to see if he was being observed. Everything seemed cool enough for the moment. He took a seat across from the man.

A waitress brought him a shot, and Ben looked at the waitress, his face saying, "I didn't order anything."

"The gentleman next to you bought it for you," the waitress said, walking away.

Darren Hall smiled. "Enjoy the drink. I figure you'll need it." He took another pull on his cigar.

Ben took a small sip from his shot glass as his eyes furtively scanned the room. A few long quiet seconds passed by.

"What was all that hostility on the phone earlier? You know, there is no need to be angry with me. I just need your help again. I'm positive that after you leave here tonight, you'll be more than happy to help me."

"And what makes you think that?" With a straight face, Ben said, "I have never seen you before in my entire life." As he spoke, he looked at the salt shaker in front of him as if it were a secret microphone. He wanted the words of denial to clearly get into the microphone.

"Benjamin, please. We do not have to go through this——"

"Listen, I don't know who in the hell you think you are, but you are mistaken with me, pal. You call me at work, tell me to meet you here. Who are you?"

Coolly, calmly, he said, "I'm the one who bribed you with twenty-five thousand dollars. Don't you remember me?"

Ben's heart skipped a beat.

Ben eased in close to Darren Hall and stuck his finger in his face. In a light whisper so no one else could hear, not even the salt shaker, he said, "Listen, don't ever——and I mean *ever* contact me again. I will have state and federal investigators so far up your ass it'll make your intestines burst!

"All I have to do is tell Judge Pomerance that you're trying to bribe me. It'll be your word against mine. There's no evidence that I've done anything wrong. Not a lick. Nothing will happen to me, but the heat will be on you, jack. You will crash and burn. I'll see to it."

Ben pushed away from the table and stood up as Darren leaned back and smiled with ease.

"Benjamin, you're not a tough guy. I know. Sit down; I have something I want you to see."

Without sparing him a glance, Ben turned to leave.

"What I have to show you could possibly put you behind bars for a very long time."

Ben froze and turned slowly to face the man. "Put *me* behind bars?" he asked again to clarify that he'd heard correctly.

"Yes, Ben, bars. Sit down for just a minute or two. You need to see this."

Like a robot, Ben sat.

Darren picked up a shoulder bag next to him on the floor and put it on the table. He smiled at Ben and took another sip from his shot glass. Then he took a slow tug on his cigar and exhaled the smoke like it was one of the few least-known pleasures known to man-kind.

Ben squirmed in his seat.

Darren then reached into the bag and pulled out an iPad and turned it on. He took a look over both his shoulders to verify that no one was paying any attention to them.

He touched the video icon then hit the play button.

When the video began to play, Ben saw what he thought he would never see. A video recording of him on the beach talking with Darren Hall. The picture was so clear, that there could be no mistaking that indeed, the person was Ben. From the viewpoint of the video, it appeared that there was a small camera mounted in the wire frame of Darren's horn-rimmed eye glasses. Everywhere that Darren Hall looked, the camera looked. And Darren had stared at Ben the whole time. Ben watched in shock.

All of the essential elements were clearly captured on the video. Darren Hall approaching Ben in the bathroom. Darren Hall asking Ben to help him. Then agreeing that they would meet on the beach again. Ben asking to see the money. The camera looked down on all the money as Ben looked at it all. It showed Ben, under the light, on the beach, picking up the bundles and flipping through them. It even had Ben inspecting the money for authenticity by checking to see if the red and blue fibers and watermarks were on the bills.

Most damning, it showed Ben handing him the memo.

Darren Hall clicked the iPad off. Ben's head hung low.

"Benjamin," Darren said while smacking Ben on his back, "you and I have a special relationship now. Won't you agree?" He took another tug from his cigar, slowly exhaled the smoke then smirked. "We have a special relationship of reciprocal needs. See, you have access to information that I want. And I have a video that you need."

Ben kept his head down.

"You get me what I want, and we can part friends. Don't get me what I want and the tape goes to the Feds, national news media, YouTube, you know what I mean. I'm really not asking for much. All I need is for you to copy *all* of the memos that are in Judge Pomerance's evidence room, and give them to me."

\* \* \*

Darren had spent a substantial amount of time deciding the best course of action for this part of his plan. He could have offered Ben the twenty-five thousand up front to get all the memos and been done with it. But Ben, based on the information he had on him, seemed rather conservative. And Darren had only one shot at this thing.

So Darren had decided to go with bribing him with a lot up front to commit a small act, then blackmail him with proof of the small act in order to persuade Ben to do a bigger act. So far, it appeared to have been the right decision.

* * *

Ben did not reply.

Darren Hall took another tug on his cigar and exhaled the thick, almost syrupy smoke up into the upper atmosphere of the bar. Laughing, he said, "Did you really think that earning $25,000 would be that easy?"

Ben remained silent.

"And you call yourself a lawyer? You're too damned gullible to be any good as a lawyer. I'd never hire you. Anyway, I need the memos within nine days."

Ben, with his face flushed, finally looked up and said, "So, when I get you these memos, you'll give me each and every copy of that video recording. Is that correct?"

Cigar sticking out the side of his mouth, Darren Hall replied with an outstretched hand, "You have my word on it." He waited for Ben to shake his hand.

Ben did not oblige.

"Ben, please, don't be rude." He stuck his hand out a little farther. "Come on." He grinned like a Cheshire Cat. "My word is my bond." He shook his hand in the air before Ben. "Be a gentleman."

Ben looked down at the iPad. The video had been paused and displayed a still frame of Ben handing the memo to Darren. With a loud sigh, Ben stuck out his hand.

The instant their hands touched, Darren yanked Ben in close to him as his face became deathly serious. In a venomous monotone voice, he said, "Do not fuck this up." Darren pulled back his jacket just a little bit to reveal a gun stuck in his shoulder holster.

Ben's nerves skittered at the sight.

"No police. Understand? If I'm sleeping and I happen to dream that police are involved, I'll wake up and shoot your ass. And then, just for kicks, I'll release the video. By now, you know I'll do it." He let go of Ben's hand as he pulled back. "Besides, it's time to earn your $25,000!" After he downed the rest of his shot, he put the iPad in his bag and placed a one hundred dollar bill on the table. Turning towards the bar, he caught the waitress's eye and said, "Could you get my friend another shot? I think he needs it."

He stood and started walking out. As he passed Ben, he smacked him on the back and said, "Nine days. I'll be in touch."

Darren disappeared through the smoky bar air like a boat on a quiet fog-covered lake. And with that, he was gone.

# CHAPTER ELEVEN
Friday 7:12 a.m. Day 12.
August 13, 2010

Ben came bursting through the door. Stunned,
Gonzalo looked up at Ben from the filing
cabinet.

"I want you to change your
investigation!" Ben demanded. Hungover, he
looked horrible.

"Son, sit down! Have a seat and relax!"
Gonzalo continued rambling through the filing
cabinets. As he searched each cabinet, he
slammed the cabinet shut harder and harder
each time. "I'm looking for something. Just
cool it and sit down."

He double stepped it over to his compact
refrigerator and opened the door. There he
found a Maalox bottle.

He grabbed the bottle, snatched the
top off without unscrewing it, and took a
swig. He tilted the bottle straight up,
perpendicular to the floor. The bottle was
half full, and he finished the rest in one sip
like it was lemonade.

He took a moment to catch his breath,
plopping down in utter relief. The chair
creaked under his weight.

"Whew," he said. "That damned heartburn, boy, I tell ya. It'll drive you mad." His eyes took on a cheerful glaze and he looked content like the world had been set right again.

Gathering himself together, he looked at Ben and said, "Okay, son. What the hell were you saying about changing this investigation? You know I just about got that lady's real name and address. I'll have it any day now."

Ben replied, "I don't care about her anymore. I'll tell you what I care about. There is a baldheaded black man, about thirty years old who is harassing the hell out of me. I need to know who he is."

Ben held his aching head. He drank too much last night, and his head felt like a split cantaloupe.

"Do you have any pictures, or—"

"No, I don't have any pictures! I don't know his address, or cell phone number! I have nothing! He has a bald shiny head! It looks like an eight ball, okay? He is built like a rock!" The cantaloupe ached and split just a little bit more causing Ben to calm down. "He says his name is Darren Hall and that he owns stock in Overton Industries, but I checked online, and I seriously doubt that's his real name."

Gonzalo tried to suck a few more last drops of Maalox out of the bottle before speaking. He tossed the bottle into the trashcan and cracked his knuckles as he looked around the room in thought. The Maalox had left a white crusty outline around his lips.

Ben tried not to stare at it.

"You've already done your own research on this Darren Hall guy?"

"Yes."

"Nothing on him?"

"Nothing."

"Son, I don't want to rain on your parade, but do you have any idea how many baldheaded black men live in the greater Metro-Dade area? Have you lost your damn mind?"

"No. Just listen for a second. He will be around me soon. I know it. I don't know where or when, but sometime within the next few days, he will physically be near me. Maybe he won't say anything, but he'll be around. And when he shows up, that's when you can get your photograph. I'll verify him by the photograph. You cannot let him know you're following him. If so, I'm in really, big—"

"Son, don't tell me how to do my job. I've been doing this for twenty-five years, and no one has ever found out that I was tailing them."

"I need to know everything about this guy. A full background check. What he does for a living. Where he lives. Any criminal history. Anything and everything."

Finally wiping the crusted residual Maalox from around his lips, he said, "Anything and everything costs money, son. It sounds like twenty-four hour surveillance of you until he shows up, then twenty-four hour surveillance of him until I find out who exactly the hell he is. It's going to be expensive."

"How expensive?"

124

Gonzalo looked up into the air and mouthed out silent calculations before he responded, "Two thousand dollar retainer."

With his credit card fully paid off Ben boldly pulled it out and handed it to Gonzalo.

Gonzalo swiped the card and while waiting for it to process he asked, "What's this all about anyway?" He paused. "It's my policy to never ask any questions, but this time I'm willing to break the rule."

"Yes, but I'm not willing to tell you."

Gonzalo shrugged the answer off and kept things moving by having Ben sign the credit card slip. "Okay. Now, when I see a person who I think he is, I'll call you on my cell to verify. If it's him, I'll follow him. Understand?"

"Yes."

"All right then. I'm on it."

Friday. 7:42 a.m. Day 12.
August 13, 2010

Noble parked his unmarked vehicle outside the Central Lab in Bal Harbour and made his way into the building. He twisted and turned down hallways and up stairs until he reached a door with the inscription on it: PHOTOGRAPHIC AUTHENTICATION AND VERIFICATION.

A female from behind her desk asked if she could help him.

"Yes, my name is Detective Stevens. I'm here to pick up a digital photo enhancement."

"James Finch Stevens, isn't it?" She stuck her hand out for a handshake.

As she reached out, Noble noticed a large, brown, furry wart on the back of her hand.

"Ah, yes."

He tried his best not to leer at the wart that looked like a bear skin rug. Although six feet two inches tall, she was graceful. Even though she was tall, she seemed to feel comfortable with her height and carried herself in such a manner that one would say she was statuesque, yet attractive.

"Finch. Detective, that is such an unusual middle name. I saw it here on your request report. Is that an old family name?"

"No."

"Does Finch have any special significance, detective?"

"No. Not really."

"You know, I've been thinking about that middle name since this request came in. How did your parents come up with such an intriguing name?"

"They just liked the way it sounded. I don't mean to cut this short, but do you have the enhancement?"

She just stood there and stared at Detective Stevens in wonderment. "Yes," she responded, as if snapping out of a trance. "The enhancement is as ready as it will ever be. Quality job, well done, as is all of my work. The enhancement is as good as can be hoped for. I mean that was a fuzzy video." She went over to her filing cabinet and pulled out a file. She opened the file and pulled out some photographs.

"What I did was break down each and every frame on which the alleged perpetrator's face appeared. I then enhanced each frame." She passed the photos to Noble.

Noble saw the fur on the back of her hand again. Goodness.

"As you will see from the photographs, the picture is much clearer than before."

As Noble flipped through the photographs, he forgot about the bear skin rug and became excited. Indeed, the photographs had been enhanced to reveal a clearer photo of the suspect, but it wasn't clear enough to make the face recognizable by the naked eye. He was beside himself, but refused to let emotion show. He maintained his professional composure.

"Do you guys have facial recognition capability here?"

"Yes we do. In fact, we are one of the first police departments in the States to have one.""

"Can you show me where it's located?"

"Sure. The database is accessible through the computer at the Photographic Digital Reconciliation Department. But in order to interface these photos with the database, you'll need the photos placed on a flash drive."

"Where can I get that done?"

"I did it already. The flash drive is right here."

Noble smiled in appreciation.

She seized the moment. "Since I have been so helpful, won't you agree to tell me more about your interesting middle name sometime, maybe over dinner?"

His eyes flicked down to the patch of fur on the back of her hand. "I'm flattered; I really am. But right now I really need that flash drive."

Smiling at him she replied, "Sure, Finchy."

He winced at that name.

But wart or not and despite her abuse of his middle name, he still found her rather attractive and his kind of woman. She was tall, had strong hands and a chin that could have been cut from stone. Oh yes, he liked her all right. But no woman, and he meant *no* woman, was worth delaying the arrival of $100,000. He was so close to that money that he could smell it at this point. He had to stay on track. He smiled back at her as she handed him the flash drive.

"And exactly where am I headed?" he asked.

She pointed. "Right down the hallway to your right."

"Thank you." He turned to leave.

"Detective…"

"Yes?"

"There is only one person in the lab, and he's gone until Monday after next on

a national convention for digital re-
conciliators."

"Well, is he the only one here in this
whole building who knows how to do this?"

"Yes."

"Are you serious?"

"As a heart attack, detective."

"I need this now." He sounded desperate.

"You know every department is stretched
thin with all the layoffs going on. It's all
about the budget cuts these days."

His shoulders slumped and his arms went
limp. "Damn," he whispered to himself.

"Detective, there is always another
crime to solve. This is Miami. It's just
until Monday after next. Are you this
passionate about everything?" She smiled at
him with eyes laced with desire.

Too frustrated to deal with her sexual
innuendos, he ignored her last comment and
stormed out of the building.

Friday 8:47 a.m. Day 12
August 13, 2010

"Good morning, Alyse," Ben said as he entered the judge's chambers.

"Good morning to you. I think you could use a real piping hot cup of tea. Looks like you had a special night."

"Maybe you're right."

"What did you do last night? Fight off all the King's horses and all the King's men?"

"No, I feel like I'm fighting them off right now."

"Well here." She handed him some tea. "Drink this. Give it some time. It'll help."

"Thanks, Alyse."

He walked back into his office and sat down as he stared at the stack of papers that waited his reading and analysis. Just then, his phone rang. The ring shook his skull like he had a pot on his head and someone was banging it with a big wooden spoon. He answered and discovered that it was Darren Hall.

"Good morning," he forced himself to say.

"I just wanted to remind you to stay on track, young man. You have a lot of boxes to look through and a lot of copies to make. So, don't forget our objective. I don't want CNN involved in this mess."

"Of course."

"Good. More than not involving CNN, I don't want to have to squeeze up on my trigger. I'm crazy like that, Benjamin, believe me." Darren Hall hung up.

"Ben." Pepper-haired and majestic, the judge stood at the door. "I looked through the motions last night," the judge explained.

Ben did not answer. He knew he had not been doing his work. Between Darren, the $25,000 and Dana, he couldn't seem to focus like he wanted.

The judge looked and sounded disgusted. "You have less than fifteen motions done, and it's Friday morning." The judge let the statement sink in. "I'll be staying with you late, every night this weekend, until we get them all done." Annoyed, the judge spun around and walked away.

Ben's biggest concern was not that the judge was annoyed at him. He knew that he would not be able to start going through the evidence room to get what he needed, if the judge worked late every night this weekend. That was Ben's biggest concern.

Ben whispered to himself, "I'm screwed."

# CHAPTER TWELVE
Friday. 9:04 a.m. Day 12
August 13, 2010

Ben had some hard days that he could remember. The day he was pulled out of class so a guidance counselor could tell him his father had just died. The day he pulled the plug on his mother. The evening that he sat down to watch the news and saw the report on his sister's death.

Those were hard days for Ben. But during those days, Ben could openly grieve. He didn't have to hide his pain. He could find consolation in friends. No one questioned why he looked so despondent. Nor did they question why he did not show up at school or work for a week or two. Everybody knew and understood the pain he was going through.

Today, Ben felt like he had died. He felt dead because he understood that his life no longer was his life. It belonged to Darren Hall. He owned it in the form of a video. And he couldn't grieve for obvious reasons. He could find no consolation from friends.

Ben had worked long and hard to become a lawyer. Literally, days and nights of work upon work for weeks, months, and years on end. Now, someone else, at their whim, had the power to do away with all that hard work whenever they wanted.

Darren Hall could involve Ben in all his dirty deeds continually and forever, holding the video over Ben's head and using it to control him like an unmanned Air Force drone bombing militia in Afghanistan, but controlled by a person in Nevada.

What if he was elected to political office in the future, or got a lucrative job with a large firm? Darren Hall would find some scheme to involve him in, and he'd use that video to get Ben to go along with him. The thought brought almost more pain than he could handle. He was convinced that his life was over.

But he had to act normal so he'd appear above suspicion. That made the pain even worse.

In addition to acting normal, he had eighteen more motions to do, and it was already Friday. He wasn't sure if it was humanly possible to get them done in time. Especially since he had a massive hangover. And he had eight days to get the memos copied for Darren Hall.

Just a week ago, his biggest worry was paying off his student loan and a few past due credit cards. A slight speck on the grand scheme of things in Ben's life. Now he was fighting to stay out of jail and remain a lawyer. What a difference a week makes.

So, in order to keep his sanity, Ben locked in like a radar on his work. He found that if he concentrated on his work, the pain he felt would be somewhat subdued.

By 5:30 that evening Ben felt starved. He hadn't eaten more than a banana all day, and Ben's hunger couldn't wait any longer for more food. He hadn't taken a lunch, because he was hoping that Gonzalo would have called.

A thought of Dana flashed across Ben's mind. He hadn't thought about her all day, and he checked his phone to see if she had texted him. Nothing.

He got up and looked into the judge's office. Totally engrossed, the judge was reading a motion. The judge had taken seven of the remaining thirteen motions, and he had determined to finish one tonight, three on Saturday, and three on Sunday.

Ben squeaked out, "I'm going to grab a bite to eat."

Judge Pomerance, without lifting up his head, mumbled, "All right then. See you back here soon."

The two block walk to Buster's Diner seemed extra long tonight. He scanned the area as he walked for any sight of Darren Hall with no results. He scanned again for Gonzalo. No such luck.

Ben sat down in a remote corner of the diner, which was empty except for him and two old men sitting in the front of the diner at the counter, arguing about politics.

Even though it was Ben's first meal of the day, all he ordered was a small order of French fries with gravy. He had such butterflies that he felt he might have problems eating just a small order.

As he placed a French fry into his mouth he saw Darren Hall approaching his table. It actually pleased Ben to see him. If Gonzalo had been doing his job, he had followed Ben and had seen Darren Hall.

Darren sat down in the booth across the table from Ben. He grabbed one of Ben's French fries and tossed it into his mouth. He looked at Ben and asked in anticipation, "Well?"

Ben replied, "Well, what?"

A crazed look commandeered Darren's face as he gave a solid kick to the shin of Ben under the table. Darren Hall bellowed, "What the fuck do you mean, 'Well, what?' Don't play dim lit with me."

Ben held in a scream, his body doubling over the table in pain.

"Did you copy the memos, asshole?"

Scrunched in pain while massaging his throbbing shin, Ben replied, "We have a problem. The judge is going to be staying late the next couple of nights. I won't be able to get the copies for a couple of days."

With his nostrils flaring, Darren said, "No, *you* have a problem, Benjamin. I need my shit on time, on schedule. So fix *your* problem; get me my shit." With his eyes still smoldering he kicked Ben in the shin again in the same spot as before. "I mean it!" Darren Hall slammed his hand on the table and stormed out of the diner.

Wincing in pain and massaging his shin, Ben laid his head on the table.

A concerned waitress approached him. She bent down by his face and asked, "Were the fries okay?"

Through the pain Ben managed to say, "Fine. Check please."

Friday. 7:32 p.m. Day 12
August 13, 2010

Over the past ten days Rawlings had spent many hours contemplating what to do about his daughter's request. It had been continually gnawing away at his conscience. Earlier in the day they had spoken on the phone when she asked, "Did you think about what we talked about in the Caymans?"

"I have," he had responded quietly.

"Well?"

"Dese tings take time, baby girl."

She didn't say anything in response. Rawlings could imagine that her face looked disappointed right now. It hurt him to imagine her like that.

Delay, delay, delay his subconscious told him. "Baby girl," he plead into the phone, "do you know what I mean?"

She let out a stifled, "I guess," into the phone.

He did not want to—under any circumstances—let Mariah down. But he had also given birth to his drug business, building it from the ground up. It was a beautiful thing to him, with no less of his DNA flowing through it than did his daughter. To Rawlings, his drug racket was his son. *Yes,* he thought, *a son that had been born in 1985.*

Back then, Rawlings served as a reliable, quiet, unassuming janitor. So reliable that any overtime went to him. Late one evening, he had received just such overtime to clean the psych ward because the psych ward janitor has fallen sick for the past two weeks. That night Rawlings had been wringing out a mop in the janitor's closet of Doctor Morris's office when three men came

into the room. Although he had every right
to be there, Rawlings's natural reaction was
to pull the closet door until it was almost
closed, with just an inch open so he could
see out. A single, inch thick stream of light
struck into the closet where Rawlings stood.

All three persons were now in the room.

Doctor Morris inquired, "Gentlemen, what
can I do for you?"

The man to the doctor's right, tilted
his head back and rolled his eyes toward the
ceiling. "Come on, doctor. Don't play with
us. This isn't funny. You know what you owe
to Mr. Haughtstaff, and you know what we have
to do, if you don't pay. Don't make us do
that." He sounded more like a friend than an
enforcer.

"Hey, are we at that stage, fellas?"

"Doc, you owe Felix twenty grand." He
said it like he knew the doctor would not be
able to pay that amount.

The tough guy talking to Doctor Morris
looked like he was about to throw up. "Doc,"
he said, "you know we don't want to have
to hurt you. But orders are orders. Mr.
Haughstaff told us to be clear in telling you
to make a good faith payment worth at least
two bones in two weeks, or we will begin a
'foreclosure' action on your body. He told us
to tell you that one bone has a value of five
thousand dollars."

Doctor Morris rubbed his elbow, and
stated, "That's ten thousand dollars?"

"Yeah, ten thousand dollars. Just have
the money so we don't have to go through
this, okay?"

Then the two thugs left.

Peeking from the closet, Rawlings could see the anxiety in Doctor Morris's eyes. In that instant, as though obtained through natural, subconscious thought, Rawlings knew he had the answer to Doctor Morris's dilemma.

He creaked open the door of the closet and stepped out, just as though he belonged there.

Without a hint of shame the doctor barked, "What do you want?"

Rawlings, confident as elephant balls said, "I can solve your problem, mon."

The doctor looked Rawlings up and down from head to feet and in desperation replied, "How can you solve my problem?" As he said the word *problem* he pointed to the door that the thugs exited through moments ago.

"It's all right dare, in dat cabnet." Rawlings pointed at the drug cabinet. "I can turn dat into money, mon. Easy money."

As though pondering his options, the doctor began jingling his keys in his hand. When done jingling his keys, he said nothing, but headed over to the drug cabinet, unlocking it, revealing the deluge of drugs therein.

Rawlings instructed, "Now tell me what each of dese drugs do."

Until that day, Rawlings had never done an illegal act in his life, but his inner-lion had just been released and he began moving the drugs for the doctor on the street. In the process, both he and the doctor made lots of money. The doctor was able to easily pay off his gambling debt to Haughstaff.

Over the next two and a half years,

Rawlings moved so much dope that he grossed $250,000. The doctor made so much money, that he could satisfy his gambling addiction.

All the while, due to Miami's proximity to other South American Latin countries, Rawlings was building the foundations of a drug empire more powerful than any city in the United States had ever seen.

Now, he couldn't decide which of his two children he would not disappoint. As he tried to find some type of resolution, he continued to plan to grow and expand his business empire. Should his daughter find this out to be the case, he could only wonder what her response would be. He did not want to lose his daughter.

He could envision that soon, he would hit a fork in the road, and when that moment came, he would have to make a choice between business and Mariah, between his adopted son and biological daughter.

Saturday. 1:40 p.m. Day 13
August 14, 2010

Ben lay sprawled out on top of his desk as
if it were a bed, knocked out, cold. Saliva
dribbled out of his mouth onto the desk. He
had worked all night last night until every
one of the motions, both his and the judge's,
were all done.

Now that he'd completed the motions, the
judge would have no reason to stay all day
Saturday and Sunday. With the judge absent,
Ben could copy the memos.

The meeting with Darren had scared him
plenty. Enough so that even if he had tried
to sleep last night, he would not have been
able to do so. Instead of tossing and turning
all night in bed, he'd put the energy to good
use.

His cell phone rang, awakening Ben.
Still groggy, he answered. He was full-well
hoping that it was Gonzalo calling; however,
he recognized the voice of Judge Pomerance.

"I'm on my way in. How are the motions
coming?"

"They're all done."

"All of them?"

"All of them," Ben answered as he rolled
a piece of sleep crud out of the corner of
his eye. Ben inspected the piece of crud
rolling it between his fingers and flicking it
across the room as he listened to the judge.

"That's just great. I've got a couple of
errands to run, but I'll be in soon to review
them." The judge paused a bit longer. "Ben,
good job. I knew I could count on you." He
ended the call.

Ben looked down at his watch and
realized that he had only slept for about an
hour. He felt exhausted but wanted to seize

this opportunity to begin copying the memos. He knew it could possibly take a long time to find them all. At least he could get a start.

Then he thought better of it. He knew the judge was going to be in sometime soon, and he did not want to run the chance of being caught.

The judge would not be in tomorrow, and Ben knew then he would have unabated access to rummage through the evidence room for as long as he wanted. So, he decided that he would go home, get some sleep, then return tomorrow and do the deed.

As he hit the door going out of his office, his cell phone rang again. Ben didn't recognize the number.

"Son?" It was Gonzalo.

A shot of exhilaration ran through Ben's veins. "Please tell me you've found something."

"Listen, son," he said hurriedly. "I gotta run. I followed you last night into Buster's Diner." Gonzalo's voice lowered. "That was him that followed you into Buster's last night, wasn't it?"

"Yeah, that was him."

"Good. Then I'm on the case. When I have all the information, I'll let you know."

Ben asked, "What's his real name?"

Gonzalo had hung up the phone.

Disappointed, Ben pulled his head back away from the cell phone. Before he headed home, he stared out the window for a moment or two, lost in thought.

Curiosity was killing him.

Sunday. 9:22 a.m. Day 14.
August 15, 2010

The courthouse was just as still and quiet as it had ever been. Sundays were generally the quietest days at the courthouse. On Saturdays one might find several persons roaming around doing work. But on Sundays it resembled a ghost town. Ben felt confident about that as he took the evidence room key from the judge's drawer. He unlocked the evidence room door and eased in.

It took fifty minutes of searching before he found the memo he had found earlier. He continued to sift through each and every box as quickly as he could. He was stacking and un-stacking boxes, then looking through each one.

Every time he heard so much as a creak in the floor, he would freeze and listen. He was so afraid of getting caught in that evidence room he didn't want to take any chances.

In the first hour, he "froze to listen" fourteen times. Each time it was nothing, but the jitters had told him otherwise.

By four-thirty, he had found four more memos. That meant five down, three to go, and he began to feel more relaxed.

Then he heard something that sounded a lot like footsteps. He froze, this time for a full minute. He had almost convinced himself that the jitters had again caught hold of his imagination when he heard another noise, this time for sure.

He moved from the far side of the evidence room closer to the door where he could hear the muffled voice of Judge Pomerance talking on the phone in his chambers. Ben's eyes widened to the size of grapefruits. He stood there as if waiting to be shot. He eventually eased over to the door to see if he could hear what the judge was talking about.

He could hear the judge talking in a leisurely manner, laughing and cajoling, although Ben couldn't quite hear the conversation.

Ben stood there for another minute or two before he took any action. He tiptoed back to the far side of the evidence room and grabbed the four memos. He tiptoed back over to the door, peeping out of the evidence room. From behind the door, his eyes darted maniacally around the room, viewing its contents. He saw that the foyer area outside the evidence room was clear.

Across the foyer, he could see straight through the judge's door and into the judge's office. He could see half of the judge's face. He could more clearly hear the judge talking, though still garbled, locked deep into conversation.

Ben waited for the judge to look away. After gently closing the door, he darted out of the evidence room. Quickly, with a cat-like grace, Ben stepped out and slithered into his office. He fell into his chair letting his hands dangle down the sides of the chair. He was so relieved that he almost cried.

Composing himself, he slid the memos into his shoulder bag. In horror, he reached into his pocket and remembered that he still had the key. He had to get that key back into the judge's desk. At the moment that was impossible, since the judge currently sat at his desk.

Ben gritted his teeth as he realized that for the moment nothing could be done about the key. He hoped that the judge would not notice it missing, and he would put it back tomorrow after five o'clock when no one else was there. He just had to hope that there would be no need for the judge to open the evidence room before then.

With that, Ben figured it was time to leave. He headed for the door. His movement this time caught the judge's eye.

"Hey, Ben," Judge Pomerance said. "Hold on a second," the judge told the person on the phone. The judge seemed to be in a cheery mood. "It's Sunday, and your work's done. What are you doing here?"

"Oh, um, I just came in to tie up a couple of loose ends. You know, get my desk and so forth in order."

Like the judge didn't even hear his answer, he replied, "You know, I feel bad. You didn't have to stay up all Friday night to get those motions done. I was going to help. I understand that you can't work full speed ahead all the time. Nonetheless, I wanted to tell you that you did a great job on the rest of those motions. Just a great job."

"Thanks."

"Oh, since I have you here, I got a call from the assignment judge today. She said that Judge Wall had a minor heart attack yesterday and he'll be out at least for a week or two. So that means we're going to do his motions as well as ours this week. We'll have a total of about eighty-three motions."

Ben almost fainted. Eighty-three motions. Impossible. Absolutely impossible.

Judge Pomerance continued, "You know we got so much done on Friday working together that I think I'll stay late with you every night this week. That way, we'll be able to get through the eighty-three motions, together. That means no all-nighters for you. That's unhealthy. So this week, when I leave, you'll leave." He said it more like an order than an option. "You need your rest in a profession like ours so you can think clearly. I'll see you tomorrow."

The judge went back to his conversation on the phone and Ben almost fainted again.

As he left the courthouse, his face drooped with grief. He felt a dark cloud of despair move over him and begin to pour hard, driving rain down upon his head.

He thought that things couldn't have gotten any worse than they were. But they just did.

It was at that point that he realized he was truly stuck in this situation. *I'm going to lose my law license and go to jail,* he thought. *The whole kit and caboodle.*

# CHAPTER THIRTEEN
Thursday Night. 10:38 p.m. Day 18.
August 19, 2010

Ben and the judge had been toiling away
all week long. Ben had worked hard to keep
the situation out of his mind, and Judge
Pomerance worked hard simply because he liked
to work hard. They almost had all of the
motions done. They each had two motions left
to do.

Much to Ben's surprise, as well as the
judge's, it looked like those last four
motions would be done by Friday afternoon.
They were amazed at the pace they had worked.
It was nothing short of a miracle. Every
night they had stayed at least until ten
o'clock, sometimes eleven.

But whatever time the judge left, he
made sure Ben left at the same time. He
would personally walk with Ben out of the
courthouse to the judicial parking lot.

The judge had been there every moment
that Ben had been there this week, which
meant that Ben still had the four memos in
his shoulder bag and the evidence room key in
his pocket. He had not had one second since
Sunday to replace the memos and the key.

Either the judge or Alyse had been in the chambers. It was driving Ben nuts not being able to do anything.

He hadn't heard much from Dana. Ben had been so busy that he hadn't responded to the few texts he had received from her. He just didn't have the energy to respond.

Darren Hall's deadline of Saturday morning would be there in less than two days.

He had met with Darren Hall last night and given him copies of the four memos. Darren now had a total of five memos from Ben. They met out on the beach around midnight. Darren Hall had seemed ecstatic. He snatched them out of Ben's hands and thumbed through them.

He had not yet reviewed them all when he straightened up and sternly reminded Ben that he still had three more memos to go. Darren understood full-well that five memos by themselves didn't meet his needs. All eight completed the mosaic of investing information that he needed.

And that if he didn't have all of the memos, he told Ben that, "All hell will most definitely break loose."

Ben had called Gonzalo at least ten times a day since his call to Ben on Saturday, but all he got was either a bubble-gum chewing receptionist or voicemail. Although temptation preyed on his mind, logic told Ben that he couldn't go by Gonzalo's office.

He figured if Darren Hall had followed him to Buster's Diner and Ben had not seen him follow him there, then he could easily follow him to Gonzalo's office. And if crazy

Darren Hall found out that Ben had gone to Gonzalo's office, bad things would happen, Ben thought.

As he drove home he ran the scenario through his mind for the sixty-seventh time that day, making his stomach churn into a tight knot. While walking from his car to his apartment his cell phone buzzed, indicating he had received a text from Dana telling him that she missed him and wanted to see him tonight.

As much as he wanted to see her he knew he couldn't. He typed back that he wanted to but couldn't. He felt stressed and tired from a long week. She offered to relax him, and he declined, suggesting they get together tomorrow night. She reluctantly agreed.

Ben had resolved to distance himself from Dana, at least for a little while. The current situation with all the motions and Darren Hall consumed almost all of his energy. Once he had made it through this mess, he knew, they would hook up again.

He slipped his cell phone in his pocket and closed the door to his apartment. He immediately noticed the distinct smell of cigarette smoke. Panic-stricken, he flicked on the light.

From the corner of the room Ben heard, "Damn, son, you almost work as long as I do. I didn't think you'd ever get here." Smoking a cigarette, Gonzalo sat in the corner in Ben's recliner. He lounged back as if he were in a beach chair on vacation.

There was a big brown envelope sitting on the coffee table in front of him.

Ben almost shit himself.

Seeing Ben's surprised look made Gonzalo laugh. He leaned back in the chair and let out a thunderclap of laughter. It sounded like the roar of a grizzly bear. The laughter settled down into a smile, revealing that he had so many missing teeth he looked like a jack-o-lantern.

Ben found no humor whatsoever in the fact that Gonzalo had snuck into his apartment and scared the living daylights out of him.

"You know breaking into my apartment isn't very professional, or legal for that matter," Ben snapped.

"I never said I was very professional and not everything I do is legal. But what I do claim to be is very effective, son."

Ben continued to wax hostile. "Where in the hell have you been?" It felt like steam was pouring from his ears.

"Following your man."

"You know, for one-fifty an hour, I would expect a freaking update, or something. It's almost been a week since you contacted me for crying out loud. You haven't returned *one* of my phone calls. Not one."

Gonzalo got defensive. "Listen, you wanted some information. I got it." He picked up the manila envelope from the coffee table and held it up like a trophy. The envelope was legal sized, two inches thick, and full of documents. "Stop complaining."

Ben stared at the envelope. "What do you have?"

"First, go close that damned curtain over there. That baldheaded nut probably followed you over here and is scoping us out with high-tech binoculars. And sit down. You're gonna need a seat after what I tell you."

Ben closed the curtain and sat down. He looked at Gonzalo across the table as he prepared his papers. He felt like a child waiting outside the principal's office while his fate hung in the balance.

Gonzalo had started pulling the documents from the envelope. Once removed, he placed all of the documents on the coffee table, face down.

Ben's hands lay in his lap; he was unsure if he wanted to know what Gonzalo had to tell him. The fear of being fear-stricken grabbed him.

"Are you okay?" Gonzalo asked, staring at him curiously.

"Yeah." It did not sound convincing.

"All right," Gonzalo said. As if he were a sixteenth century pirate he mashed his cigarette out on a coaster sitting on Ben's coffee table. Repulsed as that made Ben feel, he didn't let it show. He needed to see what Gonzalo had. "Let's get to it," Gonzalo announced as he grabbed a black and white photograph off the top of the pile, turning it over so Ben could see it. "This is the bald man, right?" He handed the photograph to Ben. It showed Darren Hall standing across the street from the courthouse on the street, hidden by a newsstand.

Humbly, he replied, "Yes. Yes. That's him all right." Ben set the picture down on the coffee table and leaned back into the couch.

"Is this the girl?" Gonzalo handed

Ben another picture. Ben had not expected
Gonzalo to still look for Dana. He had
told him that the Darren Hall matter took
precedence. It shocked Ben to see her, but he
was pleased that he had found her as well.

"Yes, that's her."

Gonzalo's back stiffened up straight as
he said, "Son, there's no easy way to tell
you this but…they're married."

Gonzalo threw another picture onto the
coffee table of the two eating lunch together
at a sidewalk café in South Beach. Gonzalo
lit another cigarette and leaned back into
the recliner.

"You mean married…to each other?"

"To each other." He took another deep
drag from his cigarette and blew out the
smoke.

Ben was not sure if he had heard him
correctly. Ben glanced at Gonzalo, then back
at the photo of the two eating. "Are you sure
they're married?"

"Husband and wife."

Ben scrutinized the photograph in
stunned silence. He pulled it close to his
face.

He felt his bones turn to rubber and
his brain go gelatinous as confusion began
to overtake him. He let out a gasp of
disbelief and shook his head. *What a damned
fool I have been,* he thought. He just stared
at the picture, shaking his head. Gonzalo
scrutinized Ben's face, as though he was
studying his every expression.

Then, the pieces seemed to congeal into
place within Ben's psyche when, like a flash
of blinding bright light, it hit him.

They set me up!

Think it through and make sure first, he reasoned.

The first night he met Dana she was so damned interested in what he did for a living. Which judge, what kind of law did he practice? Which courthouse? What floor? Which cases? On and on and on.

She had been simply making sure that her *husband* had the right person to blackmail. Ben. Judge Pomerance's law clerk. She had been sizing him up. Did he have access to the evidence room? Did he seem weak minded? Did he seem gullible enough to fall for the bribe?

He assumed that she had invariably told Darren Hall, yes.

Ben's eyes narrowed with contempt. He tossed the photos across the room.

He put his head down on his knees and covered his head in pain and embarrassment. He could not believe how all of this had happened to him. He felt ashamed.

"Listen, son, I can tell this is difficult for you to take in, but I've got to do my job. I need to tell you the rest."

Ben did not respond.

"The girl, her real name is Katherine Watkins. I don't have much on her."

Ben curled his lips as he continued to listen.

He handed Ben a piece of paper. "This is their marriage license." He paused. "Funny thing is, I was following the bald man, and I happened to stumble upon her by chance. When he met her at the café I was sure that she was the person in the picture that you gave me, but I didn't have the photo on me. All I had was the cell number you gave me, so I called her. Sure enough, I watched her answer the call, and heard her say hello. I apologize for my lack of information on the girl but like I said, she was just a coincidental find while I was following the target. However, I do have quite a bit on the bald man."

Ben noticed that his palms were moist. He said, "Let's get on with it."

"His name is Demetrius Watkins. He was born and raised in the South Bronx, New York. He had received a scholarship from Stanford University, then a graduate scholarship to Harvard Business School. While at Stanford he was the treasurer for the business club. He took all of the club's money and lost it on the stock market. He was lucky they did not expel him.

"After Harvard he was a stock broker in New York. However, six months later he was indicted by the Justice Department for insider trading. The case against him was dismissed when the prosecution's sole witness turned up 'missing.' They still took his seat away from him on the Stock Exchange."

Ben grunted. He understood why the Stock Exchange didn't trust him.

"Then, he filed for bankruptcy. After that, he moved to Miami with his wife. He had a misdemeanor conviction for possession of less than fifty grams of marijuana and a felony conviction for assault out of New York City."

"Why am I not surprised?" Ben stated.

"Since you wanted to know what his job

is, right now, I don't think he has one. I don't think that nut ever sleeps. I swear."

He took in every word from Gonzalo. His eyes darted back and forth as he tried to synthesize and make sense of all of this new information.

"Everything I just told you can be verified through these documents here on your coffee table." There was a moment of awkward silence as Gonzalo waited to see if Ben had any questions. Ben just stared blankly at the table, so Gonzalo stated, "I'ma give you some time to yourself. If you need me, give me a call. Take care." Gonzalo eased out of the door.

Stupefied and astonished, Ben gripped the arms of the chair and sat back with a blank look on his face.

*If nothing ever changed, there'd be no butterflies.*
~Unknown

# CHAPTER FOURTEEN
Early Friday. 2:08 am. Day 19.
August 20, 2010

Sometime after Gonzalo left Ben eased from his Abraham Lincoln-like posture and began to thoroughly examine the contents of the envelope—painful picture by painful picture, agonizing document by agonizing document.

Two hours had passed since Ben had looked at the last piece of paper in the envelope and now he laid on the couch, staring blankly at the ceiling. He could smell the warm, crisp salt in the night ocean breeze flowing through the open window in his living room. Hoping to help sooth his mind he listened to *Un Bel Di Vedremmo* from *Madame Butterfly* through his iPod. It did nothing to ease his pain.

His lips pursed and arms folded, Ben contemplated his dilemma. Since Gonzalo had left, Ben had imagined a thousand different ways to make Demetrius feel the pain that he felt right now.

Of all the methodologies, from hanging him by his toes to wrapping his nuts in filet mignon while he was in a lion cage, Ben most enjoyed the thought of slowly pulling his fingernails out over the course of ten days. One nail per day.

He knew that any of those options were unreal, but for the moment, it sure felt good to imagine them. Ben had come to a few conclusions. The prevailing conclusion seemed to be that no true sleep or rest would come to him until he had broken free of Demetrius's clasp.

He also knew that he had to move on beyond the primordial thought of pure revenge. Revenge would not solve his problem and would most likely make his life worse. Maybe if he could understand Dana—no, Katherine, and Darren's—rather, Demetrius's—motivation, then perhaps he could formulate a way to get himself out of this mess. He knew Demetrius had to be in it for money. That was a given. But Katherine, she was a harder nut for Ben to crack. She had, without trying it seemed, worked her way into Ben's heart.

He wasn't totally naïve. He didn't think they were deeply in love, but he had felt a real connection with her. Could she truly be such an actress that she could make him feel a connection when nothing truly existed?

He only had questions—tons in fact.

But, as he lay there contemplating his future, Ben decided that no matter what, he wasn't going to go down without a fight. That notion solidified inside his soul like concrete. In the midst of all of the uncertainty, he was sure of one thing: he would take jail and disbarment before he let either of those bastards further decide his future.

He reminded himself that he could not let revenge be his motivation. Though he wanted to see Demetrius and Katherine get exactly what they deserved, that could not be his driving force. He understood that too much hatred and negative energy would cloud his thinking, so he re-clarified his goal. He wanted to be free of Demetrius and the video, not seek revenge, which meant he had to get all copies of the video. Demetrius could have his freaking memos. But Ben had to be sure that he had every single copy of the video and that Demetrius had no digital copies.

Demetrius and Dana could then have their money and Ben would have his freedom. At this point, fair trade. Do whatever he needed to do to be free, or go down trying. That attitude, he felt, was his trump card.

All night he bashed his brains, trying to figure out how to get the video from Demetrius. One answer kept coming to Ben, again and again although he didn't like it. Katherine was the key. There was no way he could pull it off without Katherine's assistance. It was that simple.

His plan squarely rode on the quality of the connection they had. If he was right about the chemistry they had, it should work. If he was wrong, then it would be all thumbs down.

He hated the thought of such a big outcome relying on whether he had a solid connection with a female he had spent such little time with. But these were the only cards he had in his deck, and therefore, these were the only cards he could play.

# CHAPTER FIFTEEN
Friday night. Day 19.
August 20, 2010

Ben texted Dana and requested to meet her at the Hard Rock, Bayside in fifteen minutes. She agreed, and he instructed her to call him when she arrived.

Hidden from sight, Ben watched her arrive in a cab. After watching her enter the Hard Rock Café, she called Ben, just as he'd requested. Paranoid, Ben scanned the area from his carefully chosen spot near the Bayside Amphitheater. From there, he could see all traffic entering and leaving the Hard Rock Café.

"Baby, I'm here," she said. "I don't see you."

"I'm outside. Can you meet me by the amphitheater?"

As she approached, he hailed a cab, which arrived just as she did. Smiling, she said, "Hey, baby. It's so good to see you."

She went to hug Ben, but he was busy opening the cab door trying to hustle her in. She got in the cab and Ben followed.

"To Coconut Grove, please," Ben told the cab driver.

"No problem. What address?"

"Billy's in the Grove."

The cab pulled off.

"Can I have a kiss?" she asked.

Ben fired off a cold, quick peck on the lips and responded, "Can I see your cell phone please?"

A questioned look ran across her face as she asked, "Why?"

"Humor me," he responded. "Just let me see it."

When she handed it to him, he removed the battery and handed the phone back to her. He gazed all around checking to see if anyone was following them.

"Baby, what's up with that?" Dana asked Ben as she glanced at the cell phone battery.

Ben, still scanning for possible followers, answered in a plain, nondescript tone, "I know who you are, Katherine."

She gasped and her face fell blank. She turned to her side and stared out the window as the landscape rolled by.

"I know what you did to me. How you played me. I know that you slept with me so you could get information for Demetrius."

As if brain-dead, she showed no response. The pause was long and awkward. She wrapped her arms around her stomach and whispered, "I swear, I never meant to hurt you. I didn't know you then."

"You still don't know me."

"I think I know you more now than I did then."

"Know me or not, why did you do it?"

"Does it make a difference?"

"Yes, it does."

The cab remained silent for the next minute or two while she gathered her thoughts. Finally, she began, "This isn't the first time Demetrius had me do his dirty work for him with a man, if you know what I mean. He told me to use what I got to get what I need. The first time he wanted me to get mixed up in a scheme of his like this, I said no, and he…he beat me… When he asked me to get information from you, I didn't really have a choice. I wouldn't dare cross him again. And Demetrius had gotten himself into so much trouble. That meant I was in trouble."

She told Ben of Demetrius's troubles with Rawlings and what would happen if he didn't come up with the five hundred thousand dollars in thirty days. "He made sure that he was the center of my world and that I believed I couldn't do anything without him."

Ben looked confused as he searched for answers. "He told you to sleep with me?"

"He never told me directly to sleep with you. He told me to do whatever I needed to do to get the information. I knew coming back home without the answers to his questions was not an option. And after the first night I told him we slept together. To him, it was like I had put a dollar into a vending machine to get a soda. He didn't care that we slept together. All he cared about was the information I got from you. And I didn't count on ending up actually caring about you."

Ben gave a look of surprise.

"Because his life was on the line, I think he kind of wanted me to see you. Part of me was seeing you because he forced me to;

the other part of me was seeing you because... because I wanted to. But the truth is, Ben, he's a controlling son of a bitch."

"Then we both have something in common. He controls both of us. But, you know, I think we can bring him down."

"You're talking crazy. Just do what he says."

"I can't do that."

"The way I see it, you don't have a choice."

"Katherine, I've already decided that I'm not going to live my life under his control. Period."

"Do you think you can actually get from under his control? He's not going to let that happen. Ever."

"Maybe not me alone, but, together, I think we can do it."

"You're talking fantasy land. There's so much you don't know." She said as if she were about to laugh Ben to scorn.

"Why don't you let me in, then? Let's see if we can come up with something to get us from under this monster."

The cab stopped outside Billy's in the Grove Restaurant. "Sir, we're here," the cab driver announced. "Thirty-four dollars and seventy-nine cents."

Ben turned to Katherine and said, "We have a common goal. We can work together to get to it, but I can't do it without you. I need to know if you're down."

The cab driver didn't seem to care about what they had going on. He repeated the fee, as though Ben hadn't heard him the first time he said it.

"Ben, I don't know if we should even try…"

The cab's meter, still running, charged another dollar.

"I know it's a big risk. But this moment, it's a real chance to change your life. Do you want to continue your role in life as your husband's minion? This is your chance. You can take it, or——" he handed Katherine the battery to her cell phone "——you can go back to home to Demetrius."

Ben waited for a response from Katherine, who looked to be lost in deep thought.

"Sir," the cab driver announced louder this time, "that will be $35.79."

Ben pulled out a fifty dollar bill and handed it to the cab driver. "Keep the change."

Ben turned to Katherine and lifted his brows. "So what's it gonna be?"

After a few more seconds of deep thought, she exited the cab and in a hopeful tone said, "I hope to God I'm not making a mistake."

* * *

"I was so fucking angry with you last night when I found out." Ben and Katherine sat across from each other in a booth tucked away in a corner and as he spoke, his face expressed the wide array of emotions he felt. He grabbed a piece of bread off the table and tore into it.

Her eyes flickered away in shame before she brought them back to Ben's face. "How did you find out?"

"I had a P.I. investigate Demetrius the day after he showed me the video. He gave me a complete report last night."

"Are you still angry with me?"

"Believe me, I'd like to be but honestly, I can't afford to. I need you too much."

"He needs you, too, Ben. He needs you more than you know."

"How?" Ben inquired.

"Demetrius, if he wants to live past September first, he needs those memos, and he needs them, like, by the end of this weekend. This guy Rawlings, he will kill Demetrius, if he doesn't pay him on time, and those memos are the key. He knew the memos were under seal in Judge Pomerance's evidence room.

"When he found out that you were the judge's law clerk, you became his target. That's when he told me, to do what was necessary to make sure that you were the right person and that you had access to the evidence room. You remember all of the questions I was asking you when we first met?"

Ben nodded.

"Once I got the answers that night, I figured I had done my part and would leave good enough alone and never see you again. Only, I hadn't counted on not being able to get you off of my mind. Crazy as it sounds, I felt normal with you.

"The weekend before you took the twenty-five thousand dollars I had been texting you like crazy, trying to maybe, get your mind off the money so you wouldn't fall for it. But your cell wasn't charged.

"The night you took the money, I had to

see you. I had known that he had a grip over me, but I knew at that point, he had you too. And it hurt.

"And then you found out about my family secret. I was so ashamed. I had spent so much time and energy hiding it, and denying it. Then, here you come, exposing it all. I've been thinking about it for the last week or so." She fell introspective for a moment, then said, "I think maybe, all of this happened for a reason."

"Yeah, I was stupid and greedy."

"No, Ben. I mean, for like, a higher purpose."

"What do you mean?"

"I mean, maybe it all happened to open up my eyes, and to get me to change my life around. Maybe it happened so you could appreciate all the good things you have going for you, even though all your family is gone. You are a lawyer; you're not in jail, you're healthy."

"Maybe not for too much longer with your husband running around out there."

"Maybe this can work and we can both get away from him. Just tell me you have some sort of plan, please."

"I think I do." Ben's eyes darted back and forth, his mind grinding through the options he had. "I know he's a convicted felon."

"Yes."

"And I know he's prone to carry a gun."

"Everywhere he goes."

"Which means we have something to work with."

Ben gave her his idea on how to deal

with Demetrius.

Katherine switched the conversation from her needs, to Ben's needs. "I know what you need to get from under Demetrius."

Ben snapped back, "The video."

"Videos." She put an emphasis on the 's.' "He has two DVDs, and he has the video stored in the cloud. He uses this thing called iDisk that lets him save everything outside of his hard drive."

Ben listened closely.

"Ever since the SEC seized his computers five years ago in an investigation, he tries to keep everything in a cloud-based service so it's not on his hard drive."

"But I saw it on his iPad."

"That could have been cloud-based, or it could have been on the iPad's memory. I don't know. Same thing with his iPhone."

"Does he have maybe another copy out there, somewhere? Like, maybe he emailed himself a copy."

"Ben, I'm sure. He told me all about the videos, where every copy is and how he would never email it as an attachment to an email account after the SEC investigation of him. He's terrified of emailing anything sensitive to anyone, including himself."

"Why?"

"Email is what almost put him in jail when the SEC investigated him in New York. I know where every single copy is."

"Are you sure?"

"Yes. He trusts me like a well-trained dog."

Ben pondered what she was saying. "So then, his iDisk, iPad, iPhone, and hard drive have to be wiped clean? Plus get the two DVDs? Is that possible? I mean, can you do that?"

She placed a reassuring hand on Ben's hand as she found her confidence starting to grow. "It's possible. We just need to have a plan and move carefully."

# CHAPTER SIXTEEN
Saturday. 8:16 a.m. Day 19.
August 15, 2010


Ben's intestines felt like crisped toast. He clutched the three folders in his hand leaving a sweaty impression where his fingers grabbed ahold of them. He entered the Iron Butterfly Café on the corner of 6th and Ocean Drive in South Beach.

Demetrius sat alone at a booth close to the door, eating toast and eggs with a glass of orange juice before him.

"Benjamin!" Demetrius called with a smug smile on his face. "Come sit down and have some breakfast. It's on me!"

As he eased into the seat across from him, Ben replied, "I'm not very hungry. I prefer to get this done as soon as possible."

"Suit yourself," he said as he bit into a slice of toast. "But don't say I never offered you anything. So whatcha got for me?" Demetrius looked at the file folder in Ben's hands with greedy eyes.

"The memos."

Demetrius clapped his hands twice. "Don't delay. Let's see 'em, chief." He stuck his hand out to receive the memos.

"Do you have the DVD?"

"Right here, my brother," Demetrius replied as he pulled the DVD out of a shoulder bag.

"Is that the only copy?"

"Would I lie?"

Ben didn't answer as he sucked in a long gasp of air, gathered his thoughts and focused in. He handed Demetrius the file folder as Demetrius gave Ben the DVD.

The instant Ben had the DVD in his hand he said, "Bye, nice knowing you," and walked towards the door.

Demetrius proclaimed through an arrogant grin, "And no thanks or nothing." He began to flip through the memos in the file folder.

When Ben left the line of Demetrius's sight, he bolted into a full sprint towards his car, which he had parked on the corner of 6th and Collins, one block away. The arrogant grin on Demetrius's face began to erode as he took a closer look at the memos in the folder. At a frantic pace, he flipped through the rest of the documents.

"Hey!" he yelled at no one in particular. Demetrius threw the files down and tore out of the café. He headed down 6th Street where he could see Ben just getting at his car.

"Hey!" he yelled at Ben.

Ben quickly jumped in the car, locked the doors, and started the ignition. Demetrius had come within 100 feet by the time Ben got his car started and pulled out into traffic. Demetrius ran out onto the roadway after Ben's car. The congested traffic forced Ben to move at a slower speed than he would've liked.

Demetrius ran as hard and as fast as he could, dashing in and out of the cars in the street. As sweat formed over his eyebrows, Ben eased along as fast as traffic would allow. Demetrius had gotten so close, Ben could hear him yell, "Hey, asshole, stop the car!"

Ben needed to go south one block on Collins to 5th Street, then turn west towards the causeway. The causeway would allow Ben to speed away from Demetrius. Looking into his rearview mirror, Ben could see Demetrius, like a madman on an obstacle course, dodging through traffic towards him. The car in front of Ben reached the red light at the corner of Collins and 5th, refusing to make a right on red. Ben stood on the horn and the driver flipped him off.

Demetrius was gaining fast. Ben eased up over the curb onto the sidewalk. He honked two old ladies out of his way. Demetrius was only twenty feet away when Ben eased back off the curb onto 5th street. He could see Demetrius's eyes looking at him in the mirror when he mashed the accelerator to the floor and shot down 5th Street towards the causeway. Demetrius ran out into the street then stood there as he watched the backside of Ben's car get smaller.

He stomped both feet down in disgust and when he had made his way back onto the sidewalk, he yanked out his phone and dialed Ben.

"I'm off to the Feds, prick."

"You've got nothing on me." Ben sped over Biscayne Bay on the causeway. "I've got the only copy of the video."

"I have another copy, jackass." Pure
contempt permeated through Demetrius's voice.

"That's what I thought."

"Excuse me?"

"I gave you fake memos, because I figured
you had more copies of the video."

There was silence on the line.
Frustrated beyond all comprehension,
Demetrius snarled, "Ben, give me my shit."

"I will."

"Damn skippy, you will."

"But you gotta hold up your end of the
bargain," Ben demanded.

"Hey, dick, last time I checked, you
were in no position to negotiate."

"I'm not negotiating. I want the deal
we had to be honored." Ben continued, "I
want assurances that I'll have every copy of
that video——iPhone, iPad, and hard drive.
Then, I'll give you everything I said I
would. That's the deal. I haven't changed
anything."

"Okay, Benjamin. Fucking super lawyer.
I'll bring it all. DVD, hard drive, iPhone
and iPad, to your apartment. One hour,
prick."

"One hour, I'll be there."

"Fuck you." Demetrius hung up the phone
as Ben sped away across the causeway into the
City of Miami.

* * *

Ben dialed Katherine.

"He's on his way."

"I don't think I can do it, Ben," she

nervously replied.

"You just described the beginning of every great success story."

"I'm scared."

"Can you do it?"

Ben could hear Katherine sniffle and begin to tear up. "I think so."

Ben started to doubt their plan. "Are you sure?" he asked.

"I'm sure." Her sniffling turned into a cry. "I'm going to do it right now."

"Babe, be easy on yourself."

"I can't be easy on myself and get it done right. I'll call you when it's done."

\* \* \*

Katherine sat on the toilet seat as tears ran down her face in anticipation of the pain she was about to endure. She couldn't believe she was about to do this to herself. Demetrius, who was on his way, had done it to her at least a half dozen times before. The fact that she had to do it herself caused her more apprehension than she could have imagined.

She had spent hours on the internet searching for painless ways to do it. She had found a way to do it with a newspaper, but that would only make her eye appear to be black. That would not pass police scrutiny.

She needed a real black eye, puffed out, bruised and all. For real. Every search on the internet said that if she wanted a real black eye, she had to either run head long into a door knob, or hit herself in the eye. There would be no easy way around it. If she wanted a real black eye, she would have to feel real pain.

Tears streaming down her cheeks, she stood and looked into the mirror. As if praying, she closed her eyes and without putting any additional thought into the matter, balled her left hand into a fist and brought it to her left eye with all the might she could muster.

She felt shock when she heard her own scream. As she stumbled to her right she saw stars. It hurt worse than she had remembered, and she fell as she felt her legs go weak. She lay for a while like a mangled clump of dough on the floor. When she regained her composure she stood and looked in the mirror. Her eye had swollen to the size of a shot put and the color of a sun-dried prune.

Dazed and still crying, she pulled out her phone and dialed 911.

"Metro-Dade Emergency Services. How may I help you?"

"I need to report an assault."

"Who was assaulted, ma'am?"

Sniffling through a sob, she stated, "I was."

"By whom?"

"He's going to get his gun, and he's on his way back here now." Her voice meandered between a moan and cry.

"Who did this, ma'am?"

"My husband."

* * *

When Demetrius arrived at the apartment, there were five police cars out front, with flashing lights blaring.

He thought, *what the hell happened here? A murder?* What could have possibly happened to one of his neighbors? But none of those concerns slowed his pace. He needed to get those items from his apartment and head on over to Ben's so he could finish this deal.

His plan was to get the memos and decipher which of the eight subsidiaries was the one that held the valuable technology. He would then put the $175,000 into a number of AmeriTrade accounts, using it to buy the stock of the valuable subsidiary.

He then would release all eight memos on the internet. Once the financial institutions learned of the memos, he accurately surmised that the value of his stock would multiply by five within the first three days. This would yield him at least $800,000.

He would pay Rawlings his money and have well over $300,000 for himself. *Life will be good,* he thought as he headed into the lobby and up the stairs to his apartment.

As he turned the corner, he saw Katherine standing outside of their apartment door talking to three police officers. He felt surprise as he realized the police commotion involved Katherine. As he walked up to the scene, Katherine looked up at him and he noticed that she had a black eye. His hands balled into fists as he silently determined to kill her assailant. He was hoping it was Ben, but when he heard her say, "That's him, officer," he realized that something indeed was very wrong with this picture.

As though they were caught off guard, two of the officers grabbed Demetrius and yanked his arms behind his back.

"What the hell?" Demetrius blurted as he cut his eyes at Katherine.

The officers handled Demetrius in a forceful manner and before he knew it, he had been placed in handcuffs. His shoulder bag fell off his shoulder and during the commotion between Demetrius and the officers, Katherine picked it up.

"Sir," one of the officers said in a hostile manner, "you're under arrest for domestic assault."

Perplexed, Demetrius's mouth hung open.

The third cop backed Katherine away from the other two officers and Demetrius. An officer patted Demetrius down and immediately found his gun tucked neatly in the small of his back.

"Richy," one cop said to the other, holding up the gun, "look what we have here. A firearm in the possession of a convicted felon. He's going away for a bit, eh?"

Through a growling frown the other cop chimed in, "Sir, you have the right to remain silent…"

As his rights were given to him, Demetrius slouched and dropped his head.

* * *

Katherine called Ben.

"I'm at the police station now, making my statement."

"What happened?"

"They arrested him. Like you said, they are going to charge him with being a felon in possession of a handgun and domestic assault.

They said his bail will probably be high."

That gave her some solace. She was the only one who ever did anything for Demetrius, and she was the only other person who would ever have any chance at discovering where he hid the $175,000. She was positive he didn't trust her anymore. He had burned too many bridges in the past for anyone else to ever consider bailing him out. And she knew that Demetrius wouldn't have any access to bail money without her.

She figured on Demetrius being in jail for at least a few weeks.

"Are you okay?" Ben asked her.

"No."

"Do you want me to come by?"

"No, you know what you have to do now. You should get to it."

"I know."

"I left the key under the mat."

\* \* \*

Ben let himself into Katherine and Demetrius's apartment. Upon entry, he saw a curio cabinet, in which he could see pictures of Demetrius and Katherine hugging each other at Disney World on their honeymoon. It made Ben feel a bit uneasy seeing those two together like that.

He looked over into the corner by a large window and saw a PC on a desk with some files next to it. Ben looked in the files to find that they contained the memos.

He found a shredder in the corner and shredded each memo. When he was done he went into the walk-in closet in the bedroom and looked under a mass of clothes on the floor, just where Katherine had told him to look. There, he found the remaining DVD. He snapped it into two pieces and then the two pieces into four. He put the pieces in his back pocket so that later he could provide a more complete destruction of both DVDs.

He went back to the PC and turned it on.

The screen asked for the username and password. It was password protected, just as Katherine had told him it would be.

"Relax," Ben said to himself. He was no computer whiz but here he sat, about to attempt to hack into Demetrius's computer. He had done his research online and found that it was rather easy to hack into a PC that was password protected.

He turned the computer off and when he turned it back on he pressed command-s causing the computer to boot up into single user mode. He went through the prompts, and when the computer had rebooted the login window requested a new username and password. He had chosen the name and words from the slave known for leading the revolt on La Amistad.

The screen then went to the desktop view, revealing that he had successfully hacked his way in.

"Voila," he said to himself and then went straight to the iDisk icon. He found the file labeled "movies" and clicked on it. Inside that folder, he found the video he was looking for and clicked on it.

He only saw one file in there, labeled "moneyshot.wav" which he opened. The video of him and Demetrius began playing.

Ben closed that window and hit delete. The file disappeared.

He then began searching through the files on the hard drive. He found a file labeled passwords. He flipped through each file until he found one labeled, "iCloud" where he found the username and password for Demetrius's iCloud account. He wrote it down.

Next, he went to the desktop where he found the icon for Find My iPhone, which he clicked. He logged in using Demetrius's iCloud username and password. Once in, a map appeared on the screen which identified the location of Demetrius's iPhone. The computer indicated the iPhone's location as 1321 NW 13 Street Miami, better known as the Pre-Trial Detention Center, a booking facility that processes and houses all inmates awaiting trial, arraignment, or the setting of bail.

Ben hit the icon for the iPhone and three options appeared on the screen: Display Message or Sound, Remote Lock or Remote Wipe. Ben hit Remote Wipe. The screen blipped and informed Ben that Demetrius's iPhone had been wiped clean.

He repeated the process for Demetrius's iPad.

He turned his attention to cleaning the PC. He looked through the CDs in the computer desk until he found the disc labeled Boot Disk. He shoved it into the hard drive, then held the 'C' button until the computer rebooted. When the Installer Menu popped up Ben chose Disk Utility, then Erase, then Security Options. He selected Zero Data, effectively erasing the PC clean of all information.

He reclined back in the chair as he felt his ability to breathe getting easier. He had erased any vestiges of the video off of Demetrius's iPad, iPhone, and PC. The DVD copies had been smashed and rendered useless. He closed his eyes and enjoyed the first moment of peace he had since this whole quagmire began as he quickly fell asleep.

Three hours later he opened his eyes to find Katherine standing in front of him with her shoulders sagging and face void of any expression.

She said, "I need a hug."

Ben obliged.

"Let me see that eye," Ben requested. He noticed the skin on her eyelid seemed to have been stretched to its maximum capacity and he surmised that if it swelled another millimeter, it would burst open. Under the skin he could see blood vessels of varying hues of red, purple, and blue. Plump and juicy as a Muscadine grape, the word *shiner* would do it no justice. He frowned at the sight.

"It hurts like hell, and I feel miserable."

Ben placed a soft, passionate kiss on her face, next to her eye. "Does that feel better?"

"No."

"Do you want to have a doctor look at that?"

"No, I've been through this before. I just need some time to convalesce."

"Are you sure?"

"I'm sure. While I do, can I stay at your place?"

"Of course, babe." He pulled himself closer to her and held her in his arms. Eventually they let loose of each other's grasp and Katherine headed into the bedroom.

In a rush, she packed some clothes and advised Ben that she was ready to go. Standing at the door, she turned around and looked at the apartment, as though it represented a life under the absolute authority of Demetrius. She took a long gaze at it, giving Ben the impression that she was indeed leaving and would never go there again.

\* \* \*

As Ben drove Katherine back to his place, he thought, no matter what Demetrius told the authorities, they would not be able to prove that Ben had done anything wrong. The only person who would testify against him was Demetrius, and as a convicted felon, he wouldn't be received as an honest upstanding citizen, if he told his story. A grand jury would never buy it.

Furthermore, Demetrius would have to explain where he got the $25,000 that he gave to Ben. That meant that if Rawlings followed the ensuing trial at all, it would raise his attention. And Ben was sure that Demetrius would not want to have that. Besides, there were no more copies of the video left.

Ben figured his and Katherine's problem was that when Demetrius got out of jail (and he would eventually get out of jail) he would come looking for them. And that scared Ben because he was of the impression

that Demetrius no longer cared about the
consequences of his actions.

# CHAPTER SEVENTEEN

Sunday night. 7:45 p.m. Day 20.
August 22, 2010

Ben had held a vigil over Katherine for the past day and a half. He was no physician, but it seemed obvious to him that Katherine needed to see a doctor about that eye. No matter how hard he had pressed the issue, she flatly refused every time he made the suggestion. As a result, the best he could do was keep watch over her.

Earlier that day Ben had given her two Tylenol P.M. and she had been knocked out for most of the day. When she awoke on the couch, she called Ben over to her.

She spoke softly, "Ben, baby, first thing in the morning, we need to deal with something."

"What's that?"

"I know where he hid the money. He doesn't know that I know."

"I thought he trusted you like a trained dog?"

"With everything except money."

"So long as he trusted you with the videos we're straight, right?" Ben was still slightly concerned about whether he had every copy of the video.

"I told you, that was every copy of the video." Her tone low, as if she spoke too loud it would cause her eye to hurt. "Relax," she said. "You see the shoulder bag over there?" She pointed by the kitchen, and Ben shook his head. It was the bag that fell off Demetrius's shoulder when he was arrested.

"In there is a key that has 'box 207' printed on it."

Ben listened closely.

"That key is to a P.O. box at the Miami Beach post office. That's where you'll find the money."

"I don't get it."

"Demetrius, as you know, is a bit eccentric. He couldn't think of a place to hide the money, and it was driving him crazy trying to find the right place. He said he couldn't use the bank, because they have to alert the government to any cash deposits over $10,000."

Ben nodded.

"He couldn't put it in a safe deposit box, because it was too bulky. And there was no way he would leave it at our apartment. So, he decided to let the United States Postal Service protect it for him. He mailed the money to himself in seven boxes. He had told me of his mail plan, but gave me no details as to where he intended to mail it. Luckily, I found his receipt for payment for the post office box that he rented. The receipt indicated that he rented a box in Miami Beach. It's no coincidence that the key has 207 on it. And unless someone at the Post Office stole it, it should still be there."

"Why are you telling me this?"

She lifted her head so she could see his face through her open eye. "Because I want you to go get it for me."

Ben paced the room in contemplation, thinking a million what-ifs. "I don't know, Katherine…"

"What?"

"That's just it, I don't know what. What's going on; what to expect when I go there; what will happen?"

"Babe, you need to go get that money. We're going to need it, especially if Demetrius gets out. Do you understand? If I could, I'd go myself, but I think the sooner it gets done, the better."

Ben thought about it for a moment longer. He stopped pacing as though he had reached a conclusion and said, "I'll do it."

# CHAPTER EIGHTEEN
Monday. Day 22.
August 23, 2010


Bright and early Monday morning, Noble found himself in no small uproar. The clock read 8:45 a.m. and the photographic digital reconciliator would be in at 9:00. Noble would then be able to get a match on his enhanced photograph.

He pressed the accelerator to the floor. He had resolved that today was his day and his day alone, like his own personal national holiday. In celebration, he pulled a joint out of the glove compartment that he got from J.C. and sparked it up. As he drove down I-95, he listened to "I Get High" by Memphis Bleek.

Noble took three long hits and then threw the rest of the joint out the window.

He had solved numerous robberies and homicides, but after years of trying to make the world a better place, he realized that all of his efforts had not amounted to a hill of beans. Miami wasn't any safer than when he began. And of his efforts to improve the quality of life in Miami over the past two decades, nobody really gave a shit.

After twenty-two years of service, he earned $61,500 per year and could not hope to see much more than that. Today, he meant full well to collect his hill of beans. A very large hill of beans. One hundred thousand beans could make quite a nice little hill, in addition to the retirement check he would receive.

In retaliation to the munchies, he chomped the hell out of two donuts. After he finished them, he flung the wax paper out the window of his sedan.

The wax paper whisked through the air like a small tornado had taken hold of it, and he blasted past cars on Interstate 95. Destiny awaited him at Photographic Digital Reconciliation, and no one or nothing was going to stop his arrival there at nine o'clock sharp.

At five minutes till Noble arrived at the door. It was just that type of tediousness that had made Noble legendary amongst his peers and criminals alike. Two minutes after his arrival, a short scientist-looking man with round rimmed glasses showed up at the door that had the inscription: PHOTOGRAPHIC DIGITAL RECONCILIATION. The man held a book under one arm and a brown paper bag that presumably held his lunch in his opposite hand. He towered over the scientific man by at least a foot and a half.

The man glared at him with inspection on his face. Small in stature, he had to arch his back a bit to look up at Noble. "Can I help you?"

"Yes, sorry." Noble noticed that he was half blocking the door. He moved to the side as he said, "My name is James Stevens. Rather, Detective Stevens."

In a welcoming, 'you're-a-part-of-the-family' type voice, he replied, "Oh, I didn't realize that you were a police officer." He began to unlock the door. He put his book under his chin to free his hand, allowing him to turn the key.

The door tweaked open. "Please come right on in. Have a seat." He placed the book on the corner of his desk and his lunch in the refrigerator. He turned to Noble and stuck his hand out. "I'm Randall DelForio. Everybody calls me Randy. Welcome to Photographic Digital Reconciliation."

"Thanks. How was the convention?"

"Those schmucks didn't teach me anything I didn't already know. A waste of time and taxpayer money. I did enjoy the time off, though. What can I do you for, today?"

"I have a digitally enhanced photograph, and I need to see if you can match it."

Randall looked at Noble through the bifocal portion of his glasses. "You'll need those photos placed on CD or a flash drive or something."

He handed the flash drive to Randy and said, "How long will this take?"

"It'll take awhile."

"How long is awhile?"

"Oh, say, an hour, hour and a half."

Randall started walking to the side door of his office and Noble followed. It opened up into a room that held a PC on a desk that was hardwired into a database. On the side of the PC, in large letters, it read: Hi, I'm Jessica. I'm sexy.

"You know," Randall said, "the jackhammers that make up the budget screw me over every year." He sat down at the PC and turned it on. "For instance, take this computer here I so affectionately call Jessica. Jessica does not have all of the software she needs for me to do my job efficiently. It takes her a half hour alone just to boot up. That's where your first half hour of waiting is going.

"Now, Jessica, as is, is a $150,000 machine and those jackhammers that make up the budget at City Hall don't want to spend another $10,000 to buy a simple upgrade for her so that I can do my job more efficiently."

The computer made start up noises and grinds, and the monitor started to blip and bleep. He entered a password and began typing a dozen other start up procedures as he continued to talk.

"For instance, for another $10,000, assuming your suspect has a prior mug shot, Jessica would be able to give me the name of this guy and get you out of here in about ten minutes. Now, say for instance that you needed to solve a crime and the suspect is out at Miami International Airport leaving in forty-five minutes." As he continued to talk, his typing became louder and harder on the keyboard.

Noble stood there, listening, but not really caring about what was being said.

"Well," Randall continued, "Mr. Murderer is getting away while poor Jessica sits here working at a snail's pace to tell me his name and address. An hour and a half later, while Mr. Murderer is in Acapulco, I'm telling you who he is. Surprise! It's too late! I told those jackhammers this at the last four budget meetings, but of course, they don't give a damn. Wait until it's their wife or kid getting murdered. Then they'll care about Jessica's speed. What a group of jackhammers!" He looked up at Noble, as though he had just come out of a trance. "Oh, my, I'm sorry. I just get so upset about those people at City Hall. Certainly you can understand."

"By all means, Randy, I do." He meant it.

"Say, you might want to come back, say around, 10:45?"

Disappointed, but accepting the way things work, Noble replied, "I'll be back at 10:45."

Noble left. He looked at his watch. When Noble stepped outside, he noticed a travel agency across the street and made his way over there.

A travel agent assisted him while he rummaged through travel brochures for an hour and a half. After reading and discussing different locations, he settled on Guadeloupe as his first vacation destiny. Now he only needed the $100,000 to help fund the trip. He decided that once he had the name, address, and $100,000, he would rush over to personnel and summarily submit his retirement papers.

At exactly 10:43, Noble returned to Randall's office only to find a yellow piece of legal pad paper taped to the door that read: At a meeting, will be back, circa 11:00.

"What the hell does circa mean?" Noble said out loud to himself.

He paced around in a little circle in the hallway. If there was anything he hated was when something did not move forward on schedule.

Finally, at 11:07, Randall appeared.

Randall greeted Noble as he unlocked the door.

"What the hell does 'circa' mean?" Noble asked as he followed him into his office.

"It means, close to or about. These meetings, you know, you never know when the head jackhammer is going to call one, and you never know when the head jackhammer is going to let you out. He is not time-sensitive like you and me."

Noble grunted.

They entered the computer room. The computer monitor read:

ONE MATCH FOUND; 92.23% PROBABILITY.

Noble got edgy.

"Let's see what Jessica reveals to us." He hacked away at the keyboard for a couple of more seconds. "Here it comes, detective."

Noble watched as the picture and name he so long waited for popped up on the screen. A mug shot appeared with the name, Demetrius Watkins, with his address as well. There was very little question in his mind that the picture on the screen was the picture of the person from the video.

"When was this mug shot picture taken?" Noble asked.

"Let's see." Randall typed. "Talk to me, Jessica, honey."

Another screen popped up.

"My goodness, detective, this photo was taken Saturday. He's incarcerated right now at the Pre-trial Detention Center." He typed some more. "His bail hearing is set for 1:30, today before Judge Riker."

Noble looked at his watch.

He had plenty of time to be there for the hearing. For $100,000 he felt he should be 100% accurate, not just 92.23% accurate. He would go to the bail hearing and see for himself.

"Can I get a printout of that?"

"Sure, Jessica and I don't mind a bit."

"Great, Randy," he said, for the first time showing any real gratitude in his voice.

As soon as Randall placed the printouts in Noble's hand, he thanked him again, and he was gone.

The courtroom was not crowded when the sheriff officer opened the doors to the court room at 1:34 p.m. About ten people entered and sat in the gallery. Noble entered and took a seat about mid-way back.

A few privately retained attorneys sat in the front of the gallery, waiting for their turn to represent their clients. Noble hated those bastards.

He couldn't remember how many times he would have a defendant by the balls with them looking at ten years easy. Then, along would come one of these slimy attorneys, with their nice suits and shiny cars, laughing their way into the court room with their other slimy lawyer friends.

They would sit down, tell the prosecutor some shit about how they were going to file this motion and that the Constitution was

violated because this "i" wasn't dotted
and this "t" wasn't crossed on the arrest
warrant. Too many times, the suspect would
walk with little or no time in. It pissed him
off just to look at those guys.

Three assistant district attorneys stood
at the prosecutor's table with a basket
full of files. Two attorneys from the public
defender's office sat at the defense table
with plenty of files as well.

A door behind the bench opened and Judge
Louis Riker, a tall, gray-haired man wearing
a black robe passed through and sat in the
chair. He carried the looks and mannerism
of a sixty-five-year-old, plump version of
President Barack Obama.

Judge Riker had been a judge since
before Noble had been a cop, and Noble had
testified before him at least fifty times over
the years. Noble did not want to be noticed
by anyone, so he sat low in his seat. He used
the head of the person in front of him to
block Judge Riker's view of him.

"All rise!" the bailiff barked.

Everyone but Noble stood.

"Be seated," the judge said without
emotion as he sat down. He shuffled the papers
in front of him and flipped through them a
bit. He looked up at the court clerk. "Are
the prisoners ready?"

"Yes, your Honor, they're all here."

"Okay, bring them in. I'm ready to get
this going."

Noble watched as the ten shackled
prisoners shuffled in and were led into the
jury box. How ironic it was that the ten
accused were placed in the same seats as the

people who would eventually decide their
fates, Noble thought. It seemed unsanctified
somehow.

When the seventh prisoner shuffled
in, Noble felt his heart jump with pure,
unadulterated joy, as Noble recognized him as
the guy in the video. He looked at the photos
in his hand to compare and verify. No doubt
remained in his mind. He had his man.

He slid to the end of the row, turned
his back as he stood up so the judge would
not recognize him and scuttled out.

All of his life-long crime solving
experience came down to this one moment.
The result of the culmination of all the
techniques he had learned and finely honed
over the last twenty-two years.

Now.

This moment.

Here.

He had solved twenty-seven homicides,
179 robberies, 587 aggravated assaults, and
722 possessions with intent to distribute.
All of those crimes were solved and the world
seemed be in worse shape than before he
started his career.

None of that mattered anymore. The
pain and anguish of twenty-two years of a
thankless job now eased by him like water
under the bridge. This would prove to be
his most fruitful crime solved. He would be
able to see his results. Hold them in his
hand. Put them in the bank. Use them for his
retirement. He was proud and cheered himself.

Noble pulled out his cell phone in front
of the courthouse minutes after Demetrius's
bail hearing ended.

"Put Tommy on the phone," Noble garbled into the phone.

"Who is this?" the voice on the other line said.

"Just tell Tommy I got the man."

The voice on the other end paused for a second then went to find Tommy. The next thing Noble heard was the phone being rustled as though it were picked up with a bit of excitement and anticipation.

"Who is this?" Noble recognized Tommy's line-drive but bass-filled voice.

"I got him." He did not want to give any identifiable names over the phone. Noble had tapped too many phones in his time to give something serious up on a phone line. "I know where he is, and I know where he will be. Easy pickens."

Tommy let out a small grunt of satisfaction. "Meet me at the regular place in fifteen minutes."

"I'll be there."

They both hung up. Noble was unable to stand the anticipation of the trade that they were to soon make.

# CHAPTER NINETEEN
Monday. Day 22.
August 23, 2010


Tommy paced around Rawlings.

"Tommy, dammit! Wat de hell do yuh wan already? Yuh makin' me fidget, bwoy!"

"Raw, sit." Tommy pulled out a chair in Rawlings's living room. "I need to tell you something."

Rawlings looked at Tommy out of the corner of his eye and took a seat. "All right den, Tommy, bwoy. Ya know me hate waitin fah de bad news, so give it to me."

Tommy smiled at Rawlings with a relaxed, cocksure smile. "Raw," Tommy said with so much pride one would think he had just been elected Mayor of Miami, "I got the man who stole your money."

Rawlings jumped up from his chair and leaped high into the air like a chimpanzee jumping from one tree to the next. "Yuh nah tellin' me da trute now, Tommy?"

Tommy pulled out the photos of Demetrius stealing the money from in front of Mr. G's Barber Shop on 7<sup>th</sup> Avenue.

Rawlings examined them. He squinted his eyes, trying to see if he could figure out who the assailant in the photograph was. Before Rawlings could even try to figure out who it was, Tommy popped the mug shot of Demetrius in front of him. Rawlings examined it.

"It's dat bwoy," Rawlings said, almost in a whisper.

"Yes," Tommy said. "It's him."

Speechless, Rawlings looked up at Tommy like he could not believe what his ears just heard and eyes just saw.

"I shouda capped dat bwoy in de office, Tommy. I would've save annoda one hun'ned grand."

"Raw, you won't believe the next thing I have to tell you."

Rawlings, with a blank look on his face, said, "I'm sure me won't."

"He is in jail at the Pre-Trial Detention Center. You know, the jail where Doctor Morris works?"

Rawlings grunted in appreciation.

Doctor Morris. Now that was a significant name to Rawlings and his rise to prominence. Although Rawlings had not seen nor talked to Doctor Morris in over five years, he knew Doctor Morris would be more than happy to assist in his cause.

Rawlings said, "Good ole' Doctor Morris, uh?"

Tommy shook his head.

Rawlings looked around the room and said, "Tommy, yuh have me utmost fate. I'm goin' to see me daughter. I wan' be dare to look him in de eyes when it goes down. Let me know when an' make it soon."

Rawlings tossed the photos down on the coffee table in front of him and left the house.

*He that dies pays all debts.*
~William Shakespeare

*You and I ought not die before
we have explained ourselves.*
~John Adams

# CHAPTER TWENTY
late Monday night. Day 21.
August 23, 2010

When the lock to his cell clinked, Demetrius knew that his plan to get out of prison had taken hold. It was ten-thirty and everyone in the prison had been locked down for the night. So as soon as he heard the keys turn in the lock, he knew something good had to be going down. He had no doubt that this visit had a connection to his plan to hustle his way out of jail.

Earlier in the day, he had called the Metro-Dade Police Department and left a message with a detective that he had information about a judge in the Miami judicial system that was taking bribes. He mentioned judge in the message to insure a call back from the detective. A white lie in Demetrius's mind, but a crooked judge would get more attention from the authorities than a crooked law clerk.

Once the detective came, he would explain that it was a law clerk who was actually taking the bribe money and quite possibly, the judge was involved as well. He figured that jail house snitches must make

! It should be enough to get
him sprung.

Selling Ben out, he had decided, would
be his only option at this point. Katherine
hadn't answered any of his calls, and he had
no doubt that Katherine and Ben were now in
cahoots.

Laying on his back on his bed in his
cell, he had been busy contemplating his
strategy once he was out of jail. Tonight he
would cut a deal, and hopefully be out in the
morning.

If he was right about his suspicions of
a Katherine/Benjamin hook up, then all his
playing cards had been reshuffled and he had
to take his time to decide which hand to play
with whatever cards he still had left.

No matter what, he wouldn't be able to
get the last three memos, he thought. That
meant he had no choice and would have to
invest in one of the eight subsidiaries and
hope for the best. That is, unless Katherine
had found the money and taken it. If she had,
he was screwed all the way around.

He had no idea how his memo investment
scheme would turn out since he only had the
information contained in the five memos. So
then, he figured he would get as far away from

206

Miami and Rawlings as soon as possible just in case his investment strategy went south.

Before he left Miami, however, he resolved that he was going to kill Ben on principle alone. That asshole had completely fucked his life over, and for that, he would pay dearly.

With Katherine, he wasn't sure about her ultimate fate. He still had feelings for her. She was helpless without him, he thought. She had obviously been led astray by that asshole Ben. But he did know that she would at the bare minimum earn a black eye that, this time, he would personally give her.

Yessir, he had some business to handle and as soon as he got out, it would most definitely be handled.

As the jail cell door slammed open, Demetrius rolled out of the bed and sat on the side. He was ready to go.

He saw the silhouettes of three rather large correction officers standing at the cell door.

"Demetrius Watkins," one of the deep voiced officers said.

"Yeah, that's me."

"You have to go with us."

"Where?"

"To the psych ward."

The psych ward? A tad bit confused, Demetrius stared at the officers as though they would answer his unasked question. The detective must have received his message and ordered up this scenario so that it would look like a real situation to the other inmates. This way Demetrius would not look like a snitch to the other inmates. *Life can*

*get pretty nasty for a snitch in prison,*
Demetrius thought. He decided that he would
play along in the game with them and make it
look real.

"Go to the psych ward for what?"

"You should know. This shouldn't come as
any surprise."

*Perfect,* Demetrius thought. It was a
detective setting up the meeting.

"Your cellmate has told us all about
your decision to commit suicide. A couple of
guards have heard you talking about it as
well."

Shock hit Demetrius. Their plan was
so well set up that even his cellmate was
involved. He stood up from his bed and looked
to the other side of his cell and asked his
cellmate had he said such a thing.

His cell mate, a light-skinned plump
middle-aged career criminal with a walrus-
like mustache, lay on his side in his bed,
holding himself up with his elbow. He looked
at Demetrius with lazy eyes and said, "You
know you did, nigga."

The statement and look on his cellmate's
face made Demetrius a little hesitant.
Especially since he and Demetrius had never
spoken a word to each other.

Demetrius convinced himself it was all
part of the detective's plan to get him
somewhere where they could talk in private,
without other inmates knowing what he was up
to.

Once in the psych ward, the three
corrections officers took Demetrius to a
white room with a two-way mirror on one
wall. A table sat in the middle of the room

with a chair on either side. The lead officer directed Demetrius to sit in the chair that faced the two-way mirror.

As the officers left, the last one out turned before he closed the door and said, as serious as can be, "Be cool." It was more of a warning than a cordial exchange, and he wanted Demetrius to understand it as such.

Demetrius wasn't even worried as he grinned to himself. He was about to hand Ben to the police and in the process get his own charges reduced. Earn his freedom so he could get out and start kicking some ass again. Yes, sir.

He looked at the two-way mirror, and he knew that the detective he called and probably a couple more were behind it observing him. He sat there cool and calm. He couldn't wait to get things moving.

A man dressed in khakis and a cleanly pressed white shirt came in. He appeared to be in his early sixties.

"You look a little old to be a detective," Demetrius commented in jest.

"That's because I'm not a detective, Mr. Watkins."

"Then who are you?" His voice still held a tinge of confident humor.

"I'm Doctor David Morris. I'm the head doctor here at the psychiatric ward."

"Why am I talking to you?" There was no humor left in his voice. Demetrius gazed into the mirror trying to see if he could catch a glimpse of who was back there. He could see nothing but his own reflection and the reflection of the back of Doctor Morris's head.

"Don't you know why you're here? I mean the sooner you admit it, the sooner you can get well and get back to the regular population."

"Whoa. Wait a minute. I thought I was supposed to be meeting a detective here."

Doctor Morris wrote some notes down on his pad. As he ended his scribbling, he looked up at Demetrius and said, "I've received several disturbing references from people saying that you have been expressing suicidal ideologies since you were brought here."

Demetrius's eye started twitching. "What? I've said no such thing. Who said that?"

"Well, let's see. I've got two signed statements from two correction officers stating that they clearly heard you saying that you could not stand it here and that you were walking in circles deciding out loud the best way to kill yourself."

Demetrius adamantly shook his head no.

"Then, I have the statement of your cellmate stating that you tried to get him to give you his blanket so you would have enough cloth to hang yourself."

"Wait one second! That's bullshit. Someone is playing some bullshit here!"

"Mr. Watkins, calm down. I am simply relying on the signed statements that were given to me. In fact, I was called in from home tonight to see that you were properly treated. Here, read the statements for yourself." He handed them to Demetrius who, with deep interest, read each of the statements in their entirety.

When he finished he threw them down on the table. "This is not true. That's all a lie. I'm telling you, Doc."

The doctor said nothing.

"Listen, tomorrow, I'm sure they'll be a detective here to talk to me. When you see it happen, you'll know that I am not crazy."

"Mr. Watkins, didn't you call me a detective when I came in?"

"Yeah, but…"

"Mr. Watkins, there is no detective coming. I'm no detective. I'm a doctor. It is obvious that you're delusional. And quite frankly, in my professional opinion, I believe that the statements of these people are completely true. I mean, it's almost eleven o'clock at night and you're in the psychiatric ward of a prison, and yet you think you're here to meet with a detective."

Demetrius scooted up in his chair and said, "What exactly are you saying?"

"What I am saying is that I will have to keep you here under observation."

"For how long?"

The doctor did not answer; he just scribbled notes on his pad.

The muscle in Demetrius's neck became stiff as a metal rod. He scooted his butt up to the very edge of the chair. He could feel his mercury rising, very close to the boiling point. Again he asked, "For how long?"

The doctor looked up from his pad and through an ever so evil grin whispered, "As long as I say so, asshole."

Demetrius lost it. His sole intent was to get his hands around the neck of that man and choke every single living ounce of life out of his lungs. Demetrius let out a howl of anger as he leapt over the table, kicking his chair to the wall in the process. He reached out for the doctor.

"Guards! Guards!" the doctor yelled at the top of his lungs. As his knees began to wobble and knock he backed away from Demetrius as fast as he could.

In a split second, the three guards were in the room, scattering towards Demetrius who was fast approaching the doctor. His hands were out, reaching for the doctor's neck. He looked like a maniac.

The guards rushed over and rough-handled Demetrius.

"Fucker!" he shouted. "I'll kill you."

The guards wrestled Demetrius to the ground as he kicked and screamed. In all fairness to the doctor, Demetrius legitimately appeared to be insane at this point.

The guards held Demetrius down to the ground. Breathing heavy from the corner of the room farthest from Demetrius, with his back flat to the wall, the good doctor yelled, "Place him in four-point restraints in the solo segregation room! I'll sedate him there personally."

Demetrius had been wheeled into the solo segregation room, laying flat on his back in four-point restraints. Doctor Morris entered the room and upon sight of him, Demetrius yelled out, "You son-of-a-bitch! Let me out of these fucking restraints, right now!" Demetrius kicked and convulsed to no avail.

Doctor Morris with a needle in his hand

moved around behind Demetrius. Demetrius
writhed on the gurney trying to see what he
was doing back there.

"Come around where I can see you!"

Doctor Morris calmly stuck the needle
into the upper portion of Demetrius's arm.

"Ouch!" he yelled. "What's that you're
shooting me with? I'm gonna sue the shit out
of you, you know that, right?"

As the drug from the needle eased its way
through him, Demetrius could feel his body
relaxing. The doctor had shot him with 10
cc's of athropolizine, a sedative that causes
the muscles to relax and the mind to feel
more at ease when threatened.

"Doc, man, what's that you just hit with
me with?" He asked it as though Doctor Morris
had suddenly become his friend. He could see
clearly, and he could hear clearly. He felt
as though he couldn't think as fast as he
wanted, however. He also spoke slower than
normal under the effects of the drug.

Doctor Morris took off the four-point
restraints and left the room.

"Hey, Doc, thanks," Demetrius said as he
sat upright on the gurney and put his feet on
the ground. He spoke to no one in particular,
"Someone tell that ass I'm not insane. I
gotta get out of here."

Rawlings, in a leisurely manner strolled
into the room. "I no tink dats hapnen' today,
bwoy."

Demetrius slowly realized Rawlings had
entered the room as the absurdity of the
concept entered his drugged mind. Despite the
effects of the drug, he still felt tugs of
fear. Tommy and Peterson St. James followed

# THE LAW CLERK

in behind Rawlings.

Demetrius shook his head. "Mr. Rawlings, I'll have the half a million on time. I promise. I was just about to get out of here and…"

"Bwoy, I ain't 'ere over just the five hun'ned tousand. Yuh know itz more dan dat, bwoy."

Demetrius looked clueless.

"I'm 'ere for the five hun' ned tousand dollars, *and* cause yuh stole me two hun' ned tousand dollars, *and* for Bowers, *and* Joshua, *and* Fermin, and me van. An yuh blatant disrespect of I. Tonight, yuh pay back all debts."

Demetrius began to shudder. "Mr. Rawlings, I don't know what you're talking about. I don't know nothing about no two hundred thousand or no Fermin or no van."

Rawlings moved in closer to Demetrius. "So if yuh don know wat me talkin' 'bout, explain dese 'ere pictures to me den."

Rawlings tossed the pictures from the robbery onto Demetrius's lap. As Demetrius examined the pictures he understood that his fate was sealed. With his head down, he started whimpering and begging. "Please, Mr. Rawlings, give me another chance."

Rawlings backed away from him, and Tommy eased around to Demetrius's rear.

"I can make it up. I can do this, Mr. Rawlings." His whimper dragged long and eased into a labored noise that resembled a howl. Tears started streaming down his cheeks and desperation entered his tone of voice. "Don't forget the 2.3 million I made for you. You remember that, right? This is just a small

214

bump in the road; I promise to make it all good."

When Demetrius looked up, Rawlings, unfazed by his plea, stood still in front of him. "Turn around, bwoy."

Demetrius turned around to see a noose made from bed cloth hanging from the ceiling. Peterson came around and began to tie Demetrius's hands behind his back.

His howls gave way to a steady stream of water flowing in uncontrolled waves out of his tear ducts. Under the noose, Demetrius saw a footstool.

"Bwoy, we can do dis de hard way, or de easy way. I, personally prefer da hard way. But me only tell yuh one time. Get on de stool and put ya head in de noose."

\* \* \*

Doctor Morris had told Rawlings that he would do him this favor this evening. But there could be no signs of trauma on Demetrius other than him hanging himself; otherwise, he was positive he would get sued, if not sent to prison.

Rawlings despised the idea of not giving Demetrius a slow painful death like Rawlings knew he deserved, but he needed Demetrius dead immediately. So he had promised Doctor Morris to kill him in a manner that resembled a suicide.

"No," Demetrius replied. Through a flurry of tears and sobs, Demetrius had enough mental strength to assert, "If I'm going to die, someone's going to have to kill me. I ain't doin' it myself."

This presented itself as a new challenge to Rawlings. Rawlings rubbed his hand through his dreadlocks in contemplation. He pulled out his nine millimeter and tapped it twice on the side of Demetrius's temple.

"Bwoy, make it easy an painless on yaself. Get in da noose."

Demetrius announced, "I'd prefer you pull the trigger and blow my brains all across this room and get it over with." Demetrius yelled through tears and snot, "Do it!"

Rawlings had been in some odd situations before, but this one, in his mind, took the cake. Here's a man he wants to kill more than anything, and the man is begging for Rawlings to blow his brains out, and Rawlings couldn't do it, because he was in a jail. Go figure.

Using all the restraint he could muster, Rawlings pulled his gun back and ordered, "Peterson, grab Demetrius an put his neck in dat noose."

Peterson bear-hugged Demetrius from behind and lifted him, carrying him over to the noose. Demetrius didn't have a lot of control over his body movements, but what he had he used to wiggle his head so Peterson couldn't place his head through the noose.

Tommy assisted, grabbing Demetrius's head and after a few moments of difficulty, they got his head in the noose. Peterson let go of Demetrius, fully expecting his body weight to yank on his neck and begin choking him. But nothing happened.

They looked down at Demetrius's feet, which he had squarely planted on the stool. Tommy and Peterson looked over at Rawlings for instruction. Rawlings flicked his wrist in the air to say, let things be. Tommy and Peterson backed away.

Rawlings approached and stood before him, as if he were an officer inspecting his troops, up close and personal. He peered deep into Demetrius's eyes, this man, this boy, who had raised Rawlings's hopes so high, but left them sagging so low. So much of me, he thought, but so much missing. For shame.

Rawlings thought, *this is no butterfly.*

Finding peace with his decision, Rawlings at last smiled at Demetrius, and with pleasure of a prurient nature, kicked the stool away. Demetrius's body fell and the noose cut into his neck. His eyes began to bulge and as he kicked his legs, his body swung back forth. He began to squirm like a fish as he gasped for air. He grunted and used all of his dwindling strength in a futile attempt to get his hands free.

After three and a half long minutes of struggling against the inevitable, his body went motionless and the color of life drained from his skin. Peterson untied his hands when they were sure he was dead. Then Rawlings and his crew filed out of the room just as quietly as they had entered, leaving his body dangling from the bed cloth.

As they left, Rawlings felt business-like satisfaction and his mind began to move on to the next issue that might present itself. Demetrius had presented nothing more than a business problem and the resolution had been resolved in a business-like manner. Rawlings was feeling like Jay-Z and Swizz Beatz must have felt when they rapped in, "On to the Next One." There would always be some problem or issue, and Rawlings would be there, to quash whatever problem the issue brought.

Rawlings spoke business with Tommy as they twisted and turned their way through the prison, toward the exit.

Rawlings began, "Tommy, I'm headin' outta Miami, now, tonight. I'm leavin' fah awhile." Rawlings had thought long and hard about his daughter's plea to quit the drug business. He couldn't bring himself to do it. In fact, he wanted to expand. He would never actually put it into words or even admit it to himself, but deep down inside he knew that he had chosen his son over his daughter.

Tommy nodded in response as they walked.

Rawlings started again, "I need to expand. I'm goin' to Europe to look fah a base; from dare I will build some connectsheons fah a larger distribusheon network."

Tommy remained quiet, but attentive.

"And I'm leavin' yuh 'ere in charge."

Tommy smiled from ear to ear. Rawlings knew that's what he had wanted to hear for a long time.

Rawlings and Tommy talked administrative details. As Rawlings reached the door, he noticed that Peterson was not there looking out the door first to see if it was clear for Rawlings to exit. Rawlings looked over at Peterson and saw him in lala land, lost in thought.

Rawlings snapped, "Peterson, mon, move it, bwoy, and stop yuh daydreamin.'"

Peterson looked up, realizing he had been slack in his duties. He quickly shuffled over to the door and looked out to make sure it was clear for Rawlings.

But for a split instant that left faster than it arrived, Rawlings thought he saw the distant look of dissatisfaction on Peterson's face. Something in his body language seemed to show that he was uneasy. It was nothing, he assured himself. Rawlings wrote it off and proceeded through the door, Tommy right behind him.

# CHAPTER TWENTY ONE
Wednesday.   Day 26.
August 25, 2010


Ben and Katherine were sitting on the balcony
of Ben's apartment listening to music on
Ben's iPod, eating stone crabs and enjoying
an expensive bottle of Chrysalis wine, when
she asked him, "Do you really think he killed
himself?"

They had learned early yesterday morning
that Demetrius had allegedly committed
suicide behind bars. The district attorney in
charge of the domestic violence unit called
to inform Katherine about the situation. He
called Katherine because she had been the
victim of domestic violence at the hands of
Demetrius, and it was procedure to advise the
victims of domestic violence of any change in
status of the alleged abuser.

Another attorney representing the prison
had also called her earlier in the day to
advise her, as the wife of Demetrius, that
her husband had expired while incarcerated.

"Not for a second," Ben responded.

"Me too," she replied with a low, soft
voice. Her eye was still swollen shut,
although the swelling had gone down quite a

bit, as did the bruising.

She continued, "I just can't believe he's gone."

"How do you feel about that?"

"I feel…conflicted. I feel sad. I was married to him for a long time. And, at one point, I did love him. On the other hand, he caused me so much pain, I'm glad he's gone.

"You know, it'll be a while before I don't expect to see him popping out from the corner of a building, or sending me a text asking me to run off and do some of his crazy bidding."

Her face took on an inquisitive expression. "I'm much happier than I am sad that he's gone. I'm actually starting to feel relaxed." She took a sip of wine.

It was quiet for a while when she said, "I want to thank you, Ben. You were right."

"About what?"

"I am fully capable of taking care of myself."

Ben smiled, and said, "I want to thank you too. I've been reassessing myself after what you told me."

"What did I tell you to cause a reassessment?"

"That I refuse to let anyone get close."

"We helped each other out."

"Yeah, we be havin' each other's back and stuff," he joked.

They chuckled. Just then, "Un-Thinkable" by Alicia Keys and Drake started playing through the iDock speakers.

Katherine leaned over the table and put her hand on Ben's. Looking through her one open eye she titled her head slightly and said, "You know, there is absolutely no way we could have gotten out of our situations without *completely* trusting each other."

Ben nodded and with a reassuring tone stated, "But we did trust each other. Crazy as it sounded at the time, hardly knowing each other, we did."

Katherine smiled. "And you know I'm rather fond of you," she said.

"The feeling is mutual."

"So, then," she paused. "I want to ask you; where is this thing between us going?"

She knew that she wasn't trying to jump headlong into a love affair, but she wasn't ready to say goodbye either. So she felt really good when Ben responded as he did.

"I think this thing looks good. Why don't we see where it takes us?"

She replied, "That sounds like a plan."

Thursday & Friday. Days 27 & 28.
August 26-27, 2010

Upon depositing the $100,000, Noble had
stormed back to the detective bureau and
began cleaning out his desk and placing his
belongings into boxes. He didn't have a great
deal of important items to clean out. He had
lots of pencils, paper pads, paper clips, and
piles and piles of case note boxes. He dug
out the box that held the newspaper clippings
of the homicides he had solved. They were
all neatly preserved in a scrapbook he had
accumulated over the years.

For the first ten or fifteen years, he
kept that scrapbook on top of his desk. But
as the years rolled by, he would just jam the
scrapbook into a side door on his desk. In
the past five years or so, he rarely, if ever,
looked at it.

It was the last thing he pulled out of
his desk. He had been avoiding it on purpose.
To pull out that scrapbook from his desk and
pack it away really meant that this was it
for him. He was really retiring. Never to
solve another crime. Just then, he stopped
lying and finally admitted to himself that the
idea of retirement didn't come easy.

The world was just as bad as it was when
he first became a cop. In fact, it was much
worse. Was it all in vain? *Fuck it all,* he
thought. He picked up all of the other pieces
of junk that had fallen out of his desk and
threw them in the trashcan.

*What a waste of twenty-two years,* he
thought. *I'm gone.* He tucked his scrapbook
under his arm, and silently, without anyone
in the bureau knowing it to be so, Noble
walked out for the last time.

Within twenty-four hours, wearing the most comfortable swimming trunks he could find, Noble laid on the beach and rubbed his toes together, knocking loose sand from his feet.

The breeze was not too cool, nor too hot, but just right. He thought life could get no better as he reached into his cooler and grabbed his third beer of the afternoon. Earlier in the day, he had gone deep-sea fishing and the fact that he had caught absolutely nothing did not bother him in the least bit. *Just like a criminal,* he thought. He had altogether enjoyed himself anyway.

In a month or two, he would begin to consider what he would do in the next phase of his life. But right now, in the present phase, he would do nothing except soak up the sun and relax. He couldn't be more content. Someone had offered to sell him their scuba-diving business for next to nothing. It was some old man realizing that he'd had enough of working all together, although running the scuba business was next to not working. The business practically ran itself and nothing stressful was ever included. He thought he might do that. But then again he thought, maybe he wouldn't.

He had his $100,000 in the bank, plus a generous pension that paid him well enough to live like a king in Guadeloupe. These were the type of decisions he really did not mind having to make. So he kicked back, put on his sunglasses, and went to sleep.

# Epilogue: Rawlings's Plight

Sunday. Day 30.
*The Deadline Date*
August 29, 2010

The words of Mariah were now haunting him, as though she had been a prophetess, warning of the future soon to unfold. He could only wonder, had karma come back to take him away from her? How could he ever explain to her this absence from her life? What effect would this have on her? This was exactly what her fear had been, exactly what she had warned of.

Rawlings sat there on the plane, his tension easing up a bit after scarfing down three whiskey sours, so much so that his blood pressure had returned to a somewhat decent level. *Thank goodness for the false passport,* he thought. Without it he was quite sure he would have never escaped out of France.

He sat in first class with a blank, still look on his face. Although he looked like he was vegetative, his mind was working like an old butter churn, trying to solve his problem

at hand. And the problem at hand was, "How am
I gon git dat rat and kill him?"

He had planned to take a four month trip
but seven days into it, it was abruptly cut
short. Rawlings had been having the time of
his life. This was the trip he had always
planned, but never had the time to take. He
had already made some connections and set the
foundations for a bigger future. However,
as additional fare, on this trip though, he
learned that indeed, Paris was for lovers.
French women simply loved Rawlings.

Using his mind that seemed to never stop
thinking, he knew that he was going to use
this time to mediate and orchestrate the next
phase of his operations. It was time for him
to expand into other countries. The United
States thing ran like a well-oiled machine.
It would hit a bump every now and then, but
the way Rawlings had set it up, it almost
seemed to run itself sometimes.

To Rawlings, it was a work of art.
*That's my boy,* he thought.

He ideally would have liked that type of
operation overseas. But over the past seven
days he had figured that the type of operation
that he had in Miami and the States would not
work in Europe.

He simply did not have the influence or
desire to build a successful 'distribution
to street-level' operation in Europe. He
would never get all the European connections
and government officials bribed and in his
corner that he needed to effectively run that
type of business. In addition, it would take
years, probably decades to make the type of
profit that he wanted to realize.

It just did not seem to make any sense to him after thinking about it for the past week. So he had decided that the wisest thing to do would be to simply transport the cocaine from his suppliers in Columbia, to major drug dealers in Europe. He would be the middleman. Easy in, easy out, then show me the money, was what he was counting on.

Now sitting in the plane heading from France to Brazil, he thought back to earlier in the day when he had finalized the plans in his mind, and had determined to relax at the beach for the day. Before he went to the beach he looked in the mirror to make sure that his dreadlocks were hanging just the right way when his cell phone rang.

He walked past the balcony, which looked out onto the beach at Cannes, France and sat down at the head of the bed by the nightstand. As he reached toward the phone, he hummed the tune to "Cocaine" by Eric Clapton, one of his favorite songs of all time.

As content as he had ever been with himself, he snatched up the phone. "Who dis?" he asked cheerfully.

"Rawlings?" The voice on the other end sounded unsure, as if he had possibly dialed the wrong number. Probably because Rawlings sounded so cheerful and no one had ever heard him sound this happy before.

Rawlings became a bit distressed that someone would call him "Rawlings." He was in France under an assumed name of 'Walter McTree' with a matching fake passport. His teeth ground together.

"Who dis?" Rawlings asked again in a

growl.

Hearing that growl, the voice on the other recognized it as the genuine growl of Rawlings. He was now confident that he had the right person.

"This is the reporter," the man said.

Rawlings recognized the voice. He knew it was Jake Reid. Jake Reid was a reporter for the Miami Herald who, whenever he would get any news that might be of help to Rawlings, he would let Rawlings know before it was published to give Rawlings a heads up. The information always came with a stiff price.

"De reporter? What yuh doin' callin' me 'ere now, mon, usin' me name?" Rawlings tried to remain calm. After all, he was on vacation.

"It's rather important. Tommy called me from jail and asked me to give you a call."

THUMP-THUMP.

Rawlings's blood pressure surged forty-seven points. He scooted to the edge of the bed. "Aye, mon, now, what yuh mean Tommy in jail?"

"Well, that's the thing. He wanted me to relay to you that the police made a big raid on your headquarters about two hours ago. They arrested a lot of people. Let's see my notes; seventeen people in all."

Rawlings took a deep breath. He made himself remain calm. He could not lose it now. I must remain calm, he told himself. THUMP-THUMP. Another ten points.

"Wat else?"

"Well, I think you might want to know that an anonymous, but reliable source says they have someone in custody who knows everything about your day-to-day operations, and they may turn State's evidence. It will be a couple of weeks before they will be able to work out an immunity deal for this guy, but they say he knows everything. Enough to bring you down."

THUMP-THUMP. Teeth grinding, jaws tight, he gritted out, "Wat his name?"

"It ain't Tommy. That's all I know."

Rawlings remained quiet, although his breathing was growing into a Darth Vader like rhythm. His fury began to bubble to the surface. The velvet-like hair on the back of his neck stood up straight, into a crew cut.

"Anyway, they have issued a warrant for your arrest. The media hasn't found out about it yet. I'm going to run the story in the morning, but I wanted to make sure you were in the clear first."

THUMP-THUMP. Another thirty-six points. He was dangerously close to stroke level.

Rawlings did not say anything for a long, long time. His eyes bulged so hard they felt like they were about to pop out of the sockets. Each time his heart beat, it felt like someone was banging a drum on his temple. He tried to think. He had to remain calm. He used all of his energy to stay in control and his jaws were so tight he could hardly open his mouth, like he had lockjaw.

When he finally found the strength to talk without going into a rage, he snarled then said, "Is dat it?"

"I think that's all Tommy wanted me to tell you. It is going to be one bang-up front page article, though."

If he could have shot him right then for that last statement, he would have. Rawlings was ripe as a lime in a coconut.

He clicked the phone off in anger. He stared at the wall, but did not see the wall. He was thinking, not worried about the raid. He had been raided a dozen times and had been arrested twice as many. He never spent more than a couple of days in jail, and he always winded up beating the charges at trial, or the charges were dropped by the State.

The State could never get any witnesses that had enough knowledge to bring down Rawlings. Maybe a small underling, but never the big fish.

Rawlings had always made sure he was well insulated.

And that was bothering him. Jake Reid had told him that it seemed as though his insulation may have been pierced. The police said that they had a man in custody who claimed to know all of Rawlings operations, enough to make Rawlings's whole organization fall. And that was worrying him.

He had to know who it was. That was the key.

He sat on the bed repeatedly bashing his brains, thinking who could it possibly be? Who could bring him down? Jake said it was not Tommy. Rawlings knew Tommy would never turn State's evidence. It had to be someone else. But who?

There was no one else.

Rawlings had set up his operation so that no one person knew enough to bring him down. If one person knew what the right hand was doing, Rawlings made sure that person was completely unaware of the actions of the left hand. If one person knew A, B, and C, Rawlings made sure they had no idea that E, F and G existed.

Rawlings designed his organization that way from the beginning, and it had worked like a charm every time the authorities tried to come down on him.

Tommy was the only one with full knowledge, and he knew that Tommy would never turn. Never.

He closed his eyes and pursed his lips. Process of elimination. He began to run the entire organization through his mind, person by person, one by one.

After thirty-five minutes of intense meditation, he sat straight up in shock.

"No," he whispered. "No, it could not be." The vein in his temple throbbed with blood like a golf ball flowing through a garden hose.

THUMP-THUMP. Another twenty.

"Peterson," he said. "It has to be Peterson St. James."

He ran it through his mind a second and third time for verification. It had to be him. *How could I have been so careless?* he thought. Again, methodically, he eliminated anyone else in the organization as a possible suspect.

It became more and more obvious as he thought about it. It was common sense. Peterson was a bodyguard and henchman for Rawlings for over twenty years. Every drug deal. Every delivery. Every murder. Peterson was there. Every single delivery from Columbia. Every single contact in Santo

Domingo. He knew. Rawlings never asked for his opinion, or had him do anything important like Tommy, but Peterson had watched and seen everything like a deaf mute fly on the wall. He had seen and heard it all.

Slowly, like drying blood, the thought solidified in his mind. Drops of sweat began to leak out of every pore in Rawlings's skin. He had a lot of thinking to do and so he tried as best he could to remain calm. No one was there to clean up after him if he screwed up. He needed to remain calm.

He did everything he could to sit still and let his angst subside. But mutinously, his lip twitched and all at once, Rawlings exploded.

With a holler that sounded like a whipped horse, he slapped the night-light off the nightstand, hurling it onto the floor, busting it into little pieces. An errant dreadlock poked him in the eye. He lifted the night stand up and threw it out of the balcony, landing near some famous European actor and smashing on the sidewalk next to him.

That had not spent enough angry energy. Rawlings looked for something else to desecrate. Flexing every angry muscle in his body, Rawlings grabbed the bottom of the brass bed frame and lifted it. With a loud holler, Rawlings flipped the bed over, putting a hole in the wall such that Rawlings was able to see the toilet in the next room.

He breathed heavily as he looked at the mess he had made.

There.

For now, that would let some steam off.

Although what he really wanted to do was kill someone, the bed would have to do. He had vented. Now, he had to begin planning his next move.

Shortly thereafter he began packing his bags. He knew that now was the time to invoke the escape plan he had devised over twenty years ago.

He went to a bank and had all of his money wired to Brazilian banks. Then he rushed to the airport and got the very next flight to Brazil. Once he arrived there, he planned to father a child with a Brazilian woman.

That way he knew that if the United States ever found him, under Brazilian law, the U.S. would not be permitted extradite him until his child turned eighteen years old. And when that child turned eighteen, he figured he would just have another child.

And that would keep him out of jail for at least thirty-six years. Would Mariah ever forgive him?

Hopefully, things would not have to go that far. His time in Brazil would be short he hoped, because all he had to do was get someone to take care of Peterson. Then he could go back to business as usual.

The airplane engines smoothly whispered a constant roar as Rawlings sat in row two, lost in thought. When the plane landed he knew he had to do some work and call in some favors.

He knew it would take a lot of favors to get Peterson. But he figured it was simple as this: if it takes all of his money, all of his power, and all of his influence, Peterson

St. James will never make it to trial alive.
But that is another story.

# Reading Group Discussion Questions

1. It is widely accepted that going through desperate times together can make a bond between two people that lasts a lifetime. Do you believe what Ben and Katherine/Dana went through will be enough to keep them together for life?

2. There are a number of quotes throughout the book by a number of famous persons. Can you apply each quote to the novel and explain why each quote was cited?

3. What did you think was the most suspenseful moment in the novel?

4. What made you feel the most uncomfortable in the novel? Why? Do you believe that you can analyze this uncomfortable feeling to bring about some awareness or understanding to some aspect of your life that you had not previously considered?

5. In what ways do the events in the book reveal evidence of the authors view on life?

6. How do you think Mariah will react once she learns that Rawlings has fled to Brazil? Will she try to help her father or will she

disassociate herself from him? Why?

7. Were you satisfied with the ending?

8. Do you believe that Katherine/Dana was easily influenced or a strong minded character? Why?

9. Did you perceive any specific underlying themes throughout the novel, including the butterfly theme? How did the butterfly theme apply to the characters in the book, if at all?

10. Did you ever feel sorry for Demetrius?

CPSIA information can be obtained at www.ICGtesting.com
Printed in the USA
LVOW041402140212

268660LV00001B/16/P